He could, she supposed, be an AWOL soldier.

A criminal on the lam. A serial killer. A witness in the protection program. A deadbeat dad evading child support payments.

Her instincts told her Will was none of those things. She'd seen him with her residents and Crackers, her therapy dog. He was innately good and kind.

But something had caused him to close himself off from people. Something harsh and heartbreaking. If she weren't afraid of appearing nosy or gossipy, she'd prod Will's boss, the new owner of the Gold Nugget Ranch, for answers.

"Next time perhaps?" Miranda dropped another hint even though Will never took them. "Nell's constantly cooking up sinfully delicious dishes with far too many calories. I swear I've gained five pounds this past week alone."

He took her in from head to toe and, for a fraction of a second, his gaze heated. "You look fine."

It was the most emotion Miranda had ever seen him show, and a shiver of awareness wound slowly through her.

She inched closer. "Are you the flatterer."

Dear Reader,

Story ideas can come to me at the strangest times and from the most unusual sources. Often when I'm in the middle of a completely different book or series. I file these ideas away, hoping and waiting for the day when I get the chance to use them. That day can take years.

Such was the case with *His Christmas Sweetheart,* book two in my Sweetheart, Nevada series. For at least a decade I've wanted to write a heroine who owns and operates an elder care group home. Miranda Staley is the kind of individual I want to be—smart, caring, resourceful and with a huge personality to match her incredible smile. Her elder care home is full of quirky senior citizens who liven up the place while bringing a touch of humor and tenderness to the story. Vivacious Miranda is the perfect match for loner Will Dessaro, a man suffering from acute post-traumatic stress disorder. She's faced with a difficult challenge, that of convincing him they're deserving of their own happily ever after. I can't blame him for doubting—their relationship does seem improbable.

I had a really fun time pushing and prodding these two stubborn individuals and getting them to discover that no obstacle is impossible to overcome when it comes to love. Be sure to look for book three, *Most Eligible Sheriff,* coming out this spring.

Warmest wishes,

Cathy McDavid

P.S. I love hearing from readers. Visit my website at www.cathymcdavid.com and drop me a line.

HIS CHRISTMAS SWEETHEART

—

CATHY MCDAVID

HARLEQUIN® AMERICAN ROMANCE®

Recycling programs
for this product may
not exist in your area.

ISBN-13: 978-0-373-75478-6

HIS CHRISTMAS SWEETHEART

Printed in U.S.A.

www.Harlequin.com

ABOUT THE AUTHOR

Cathy makes her home in Scottsdale, Arizona, near the breathtaking McDowell Mountains, where hawks fly overhead, javelina traipse across her front yard and mountain lions occasionally come calling. She embraced the country life at an early age, acquiring her first horse in eighth grade. Dozens of horses followed through the years, along with mules, an obscenely fat donkey, chickens, ducks, goats and a potbellied pig who had her own swimming pool. Nowadays, two spoiled dogs and two spoiled-er cats round out the McDavid pets. Cathy loves contemporary and historical ranch stories and often incorporates her own experiences into her books.

When not writing, Cathy and her family and friends spend as much time as they can at her cabin in the small town of Young. Of course, she takes her laptop with her on the chance inspiration strikes.

Books by Cathy McDavid

HARLEQUIN AMERICAN ROMANCE

1168—HIS ONLY WIFE
1197—THE FAMILY PLAN
1221—COWBOY DAD
1264—WAITING FOR BABY
1294—TAKING ON TWINS
1307—THE ACCIDENTAL SHERIFF
1318—DUSTY: WILD COWBOY
1345—THE COMEBACK COWBOY
1365—LAST CHANCE COWBOY*
1384—HER COWBOY'S CHRISTMAS WISH*
1397—BABY'S FIRST HOMECOMING*
1409—AIDAN: LOYAL COWBOY
1441—COWBOY FOR KEEPS*
1458—THE RANCHER'S HOMECOMING**

*Mustang Valley
**Sweetheart, Nevada

To Rob, my PTSD guru. Thanks again for all your spot-on advice and for pointing me in the right direction.

Chapter One

The front door to Harmony House swung open before he had a chance to knock.

Fist raised, he stared at Nell, the part-time caregiver.

"Will Dessaro, you gave me start." Laughing good-naturedly, she stepped back to allow him entry. Short, ebony-skinned and possessing an endless supply of patience, Nell helped run the elder-care group home. "Guess I'm not the only one. You look as if you've seen a ghost."

Nothing could be truer. Will saw a ghost every time he visited.

"I'm not bothering you?" he asked, removing his cowboy hat.

"Nonsense. You're always welcome here. Mrs. Litey loves seeing you, and she's such a lamb after you leave. For a few hours. Or a day. Then…" The unfinished sentence was followed by a shrug. "She's a pistol, that one."

"Yes, ma'am."

Will had witnessed the octogenarian's normally cantankerous nature more than once when she hadn't realized he was in the room. Describing her as a pistol was being kind. Acute Alzheimer's did that to a person, he supposed.

Nell ushered him into the main room, where a couple sat together watching a loudly blaring TV, the frail-looking woman wheelchair bound. Babs and her gentleman friend,

Arthur. He called on her almost daily—and stayed all day from what Will could gather.

Sounding the alarm several beats late, a white terrier mix jumped down from his favorite roost atop Mr. Lexington's lap. Obviously hard of hearing, Mr. Lexington dozed in one of three recliners. The dog trotted over for a sniff, his scraggly tail wagging.

Will bent and scratched him behind the ears. "Hey, buddy."

"Let me check on Mrs. Litey before I take you back," Nell said. "Just in case she's indisposed."

Will straightened and nodded at Babs and Arthur. He was always more comfortable with animals than people. Horses especially, but dogs and cats, too. His own shepherd mix waited patiently in his pickup parked out front.

"Afternoon to you, young fellow." Arthur released Babs's hand to operate the remote control. Lowering the TV's volume, he rose with telltale arthritic stiffness and greeted Will. "How's the world treating you?"

"Good."

"Keeping busy? I hear business is picking up at the Gold Nugget."

"Some."

Will didn't elaborate. He seldom talked much, preferring to listen—which he did as Arthur reminisced about the guest ranch where Will was employed as livestock foreman, trail guide, farrier and all-around hand. Whatever his boss required of him.

The ranch, one of the more famous landmarks of Sweetheart, Nevada, was originally built in the 1960s and was used as a film location for the wildly popular TV Western *The Forty-Niners.* After the show ceased production, the ranch was opened to the public. Mrs. Litey had served as curator, tour guide and resident authority on local history all that time, until her Alzheimer's had advanced and the ranch had closed.

"Miranda's not here," Arthur said, "if you're hoping to find her."

"I'm not."

He waggled his bushy gray brows and elbowed Will in the ribs. "I would be, if I were you. She's pretty easy on the eyes, even for eyes as old as mine."

Will generally avoided Miranda Staley, the owner and operator of Sweetheart's only senior-care facility. She made him nervous. People in general made Will nervous, but her especially. And it wasn't just all those curves packed into her petite body.

She lit up any room she entered, drawing the attention of everyone present. Will, on the other hand, preferred to go unnoticed, and usually did. Except at Harmony House, where the close quarters made escaping attention impossible.

He usually dropped by to visit Mrs. Litey in the early afternoon. Miranda ran her errands then, and he was less likely to cross paths with her, as had happened before. Often. As pretty as she was bubbly, she had an uncanny ability to tie his tongue in knots, which didn't fare well for someone who spoke only when necessary.

Thinking of her caused his heart to race and his lungs to work overtime.

Easy does it. Just breathe. In and out. That's right.

The mantra had no effect. Angling his body away from the room's other occupants, he removed his jacket and reached underneath the cuff on his left sleeve, snapping the rubber band around his wrist. Once. Twice. Three times. The sharp stinging helped him to focus. Focusing enabled him to relax.

There would be no panic attack today. At least not here.

"I said, Mrs. Litey's been having fits all morning. Did you hear me?"

Will blinked himself back to the present and turned to face Arthur and Babs. It was hard not to think of them as cute, even for someone as unsentimental as Will. When asked, he blamed his preference for keeping his distance on a six-year stint in the army. Easier that way. No one liked talking about death and guilt and emotional disabilities. Will sure didn't.

"You go in there and work whatever magic it is you do." Arthur chuckled. "Maybe then we can watch the rest of Babs's show without Mrs. Litey hollering and carrying on."

"I'll do my best, sir."

Nell returned, all smiles. "She's waiting for you. I'll bring some tea."

Will made his way down the familiar hallway to the residents' bedrooms. Mrs. Litey's was the second on the right.

She and Babs had private rooms, while Mr. Lexington and Himey shared what had once been the master suite. There had been a fifth resident, but his family had recently relocated him to a facility near Lake Tahoe, citing that Sweetheart was no longer a safe place.

They had their reasons. A lot of people had left when, this past summer, a forest fire had leaped a ravine, ran amok and nearly destroyed the town.

Will paused briefly at a closed door. Behind it were stairs leading to a converted attic suite: bedroom, bath and a sitting area. Miranda's quarters.

He'd never been up there, had only heard about it from Arthur and Babs.

The day of the fire and evacuation, Miranda had come running down those stairs, carting a suitcase. Face flushed with fear and exertion, she'd looked at him as if she didn't recognize him, which was probably the case. Will flew miles beneath her radar.

The same couldn't be said about her. He'd bumped into Miranda on his first day in town, in an aisle at the general store, and had kept her in *his* radar ever since.

Thoughts of Miranda started his heart racing again, and he repeated the mantra.

At the doorway to Mrs. Litey's room, he stopped and waited. Someone, Nell probably, had opened the drapes. Late November sunshine filled every corner. Though clean and tidy and now well lit, the room clearly belonged to an ill person. Rails on the bed, a walker beside the dresser, call button within easy reach and a lingering antiseptic smell were a few of the signs.

Mrs. Litey stood facing the window. Will thought she might be oblivious to the world, as sometimes happened. Suddenly she pivoted. At the sight of him, her wrinkled face erupted in a delighted grin.

"You're here." Feeble arms extended, her gait unsteady, she started toward him, ignoring the walker.

Will hurried to meet her halfway, afraid she might fall. She collapsed into his arms and cried with joy. He held her, stroking her bony back and murmuring soothing words.

It was the same every time he visited her.

"Joseph." She stared up at him, tears in her eyes, and cradled his cheek in her gnarled hand. "You're home. I've missed you so much."

"Yes, ma'am."

"Ma'am! So polite. The army has certainly taught you manners."

"Yes, ma'am." He hesitated. "Mom."

"Oh, honey." She hugged him close, her thin frame no larger than that of a young girl. "How long is your leave?"

Will answered as he always did. "Three days."

"That's all? We'll spend every minute of it together. Are you hungry? I can make some sandwiches." She scanned the room, confusion clouding her features. The next instant she brightened and tugged on his Western-cut shirt. "They're not feeding you enough. Look how this uniform hangs on you. No worries. I'll fatten you up while you're home."

Nell slipped quietly into the room and set a tray on the bedside table. It held a pot of tea, two mugs and a plate of sugar cookies. After giving Will a wink, she disappeared.

"I ate earlier, Mom," Will said. "But I wouldn't mind some tea."

Another moment of confusion, then Mrs. Litey spotted the tray with the tea and cookies. "I have a fresh pot."

Will insisted on helping to pour. They sat in a pair of chairs by the window. Mrs. Litey chatted amiably, asking Will questions about his current tour. He answered as best he could. How her son, Joseph, might have answered had he not died thirty years ago in a training accident when the armored personnel carrier he was commanding flipped on a patch of black ice.

Will didn't know why Mrs. Litey took one look at him and decided he was her son. Perhaps through her haze, she'd sensed his military background. He really didn't care.

Sitting in the too-small chair, listening to her ramble, he let the present slide away.

It was then he saw the ghost. His late grandmother.

Closing his eyes, he was transported back in time to his grandmother's kitchen on her farm outside of Fort Scott, Kansas. The sugar cookies were fresh from the oven, not store-bought from a box. Mrs. Litey's voice became deeper, warmer, resembling his grandmother's. She was inquiring about school and baseball practice and what colleges he'd applied to.

In a world that had been chaos for far too long, Will was finally at peace, his demons temporarily silenced. Mrs. Litey's, too, he imagined. It was the reason he visited her and why he let her believe he was her son.

They were a pair, each of them escaping the memories of an unhappy past by taking solace in one another.

A noise from another part of the house traveled down the hall to Will. Then Arthur called hello to Miranda.

She was here!

Will cast about for an escape route, knowing there was none. He'd have to leave the same way he came in. Let her bubbly personality wash over him. Fend off her attempts to know him better. Remind him of the love he'd once had and lost because of his PTSD.

"Mom, I need to go." He pushed to his feet.

"So soon?" Mrs. Litey's voice trailed off as fragments of clarity returned.

Will kissed her cheek. She didn't respond. Sad as her distance made him feel, it was easier to handle than when she clung to him, begging him to stay.

"See you soon," he whispered and patted her shoulder. Then he started for the door—only to come up short.

Miranda stood not five feet in front of him, a hand pressed lightly to her heart, an aren't-you-sweet smile on her face. The panic he'd staved off earlier returned, and for one paralyzing moment he feared his coping techniques would fail him.

Miranda grinned broadly. Will Dessaro was absolutely adorable when flustered—and he was flustered a lot around her.

To be honest, she enjoyed her share of admiring glances from men. Had even plied her charms on occasion to elicit them. The bold, sometimes shameless, looks flattered her. But they were nothing compared to the thrill that Will's undisguised longing gave her.

How had she coexisted in the same town with him for all these years and not noticed him?

Then came the day of the fire, and the order to evacuate

within two hours. He'd shown up on her doorstep—strong, silent, capable—and provided the help she'd needed to rally and load her five frightened and uncooperative residents into the van.

She couldn't have done it without him. And he'd been visiting Mrs. Litey regularly ever since.

Thank the Lord her house had been spared. The same couldn't be said for several hundred other homes and buildings in Sweetheart, including many on her own street. Her beautiful and quaint hometown had been brought to its knees in a matter of hours and still hadn't recovered five months later.

"I hate to impose…" Miranda glanced over her shoulder, making sure Will had accompanied her into the kitchen. It was empty, her part-time helper Nell attending to the residents and their afternoon medications. "There's a leak in the pipe under the sink. The repairman can't fit me in his schedule till Monday, and the leak's worsening by the hour." She paused. "You're good with tools, aren't you?"

"Good enough." He blushed.

Sweet heaven, he was a cutie.

Wavy brown hair that insisted on falling rakishly over one brow. Dark eyes. Cleft in his chin. Breathtakingly tall. He towered above her five-foot-three frame.

If only he'd respond to one of the many dozen hints she'd dropped and ask her on a date.

"Do you mind taking a peek for me?" She gestured toward the open cabinet doors beneath the sink. "I'd really appreciate it."

"Sure." His gaze went to the toolbox on the floor. "You have an old towel or pillow I can use?"

That had to be the longest sentence he'd ever uttered in her presence.

"Be right back." She returned shortly with an old beach towel folded in a large square.

By then Will had set his cowboy hat on the table and had rolled up his sleeves to his elbows.

Nice arms, she noted. Tanned, lightly dusted with hair and corded with muscles.

Handing him the towel, she indicated the rubber band on his left wrist. "What's that?"

"Nothing."

"I do the same thing."

He stared at her.

"Find rubber bands and put them on my wrist. Never know when you'll need one."

"Yeah." He was back to monotone answers.

Miranda didn't mind. Words weren't the only way to communicate. She flashed him another brilliant smile.

His blush deepened.

Excellent. Message sent and received.

Will dug through the toolbox and selected a wrench. Laying the towel down in front of the cabinet she'd cleared out in preparation, he sat on it and then rolled onto his back, adjusting his long body until he was half in, half out of the cabinet.

"Water turned off?"

"Did that when I first got home."

Miranda knelt on the floor beside him and, for the first time, got a good look at the large silver belt buckle he wore.

U.S. Army. Not a rodeo event.

That answered some questions. She'd often wondered how he was able to effectively play the part of Mrs. Litey's late son. Where, then, had he learned to be such a first-rate cowboy?

"How long were you in for?" she asked.

He stilled. "Pardon?"

"The army. How long?"

"Six years."

"Where did you serve?" she persisted.

"Overseas."

"The Middle East?"

"Some. Also stateside."

He was certainly a challenge. Luckily Miranda didn't give up easily.

Minutes of silence passed, then a low grunt, a loud thud and a softly spoken curse word.

"Everything all right?" Miranda leaned her head down to peer under the sink.

"The fitting's frozen."

"I have some pipe-joint compound." She reached for the jar in the toolbox.

"Don't need it." His arms strained, she swore to the point of breaking, only to relax. "Done."

"Really? The leak's fixed?" The pipes were as old as the house, and she'd expected the repair to take considerably longer. He really was strong.

"Keep the appointment with the plumber. What I did is only temporary." Will pushed out from beneath the sink and sat up. Because of her proximity to him, they were nearly face-to-face.

Miranda couldn't be more pleased, and tilted her head appealingly. "Thank you. Don't know what I would have done without your help."

She'd said something similar to him the day of the fire, after he'd coaxed her residents into the van and calmed their fears, when nothing she'd said or done had worked. In relief and gratitude, she'd thrown her arms around his neck and kissed his cheek. She'd been wanting to do the same ever since.

Kiss him, not evacuate her residents.

"No problem." He swallowed.

She wondered if he was remembering that day, too. "Someone who works as hard as you deserves a reward."

His eyes widened a fraction and a thin sheen of sweat appeared on his forehead.

"Can I get you a cold drink or a snack? Nell made some cherry cobbler for dessert. I'm sure I can sneak you a piece without her getting mad."

"I have to get back to the ranch."

"One small piece?"

"Thanks, but no." He scooted forward and stood.

Miranda had no choice but to give him room. To her surprise, his hand appeared in front of her face.

She took it and let him pull her to her feet, noting his calluses. A working man's hand. Like her foster father's. She found comfort in that.

"Such a gentleman."

He met her glance briefly before turning away.

A warm glow bloomed inside her. His severe shyness, as much as his good looks, had kept her intrigued and putting herself in his path at every opportunity these past five months. There was also something about him, a complexity, a depth, a sensitivity that most women probably missed.

Dropping the wrench into the toolbox, he retrieved the towel from the floor.

"Where can I throw this?"

"I'll take it." She did, and her attention was drawn again to the rubber band on his wrist.

Odd habit for a man, she mused. Miranda had picked hers up from her foster mother, the queen of practicality and thriftiness.

But then Will was a person of many odd habits. And mystery. She'd asked around after the fire. Few knew him, none well, and no one had any idea where he'd come from or what he'd done before arriving in Sweetheart. Besides serving in the army, which he'd confirmed today.

He could, she supposed, be an AWOL soldier. A criminal on the lam. A serial killer. A witness in the protection program. A deadbeat dad evading child-support payments.

Her instincts told her Will was none of those things. She'd seen him with her residents and Crackers, her therapy dog. Will was innately good and kind.

But something had caused him to close himself off from people. Something harsh and heartbreaking. If she wasn't afraid of appearing nosy or gossipy, she'd prod Will's boss, the new owner of the Gold Nugget Ranch, for answers.

"Next time, perhaps?" Miranda dropped another hint, even though Will never took them. "Nell's constantly cooking up delicious dishes with far too many calories. I swear I've gained five pounds this past week alone."

He took her in from head to toe and, for a fraction of a second, his gaze heated. "You look fine."

It was the most emotion Miranda had ever seen him show, and a shiver of awareness wound slowly through her.

She inched closer. "Aren't you the flatterer."

Grabbing his hat off the table, he all but stumbled out of the kitchen in his haste to depart.

She saw him to the door, but he was three steps ahead of her and barely acknowledged Arthur's booming goodbye and Babs's wave. Mr. Lexington and Crackers didn't so much as stir from their place in the recliner.

Miranda returned to the kitchen, feeling quite satisfied with herself. *Finally* she'd gotten a reaction from Will. A small one, but there was no mistaking it. He was interested in her, and that was enough for now.

She had considered being less intimidating—her big personality didn't appeal to everyone—only to change her mind. Will seemed to like her plenty fine the way she was, despite his wariness.

Nell came into the kitchen just as Miranda was closing the lid on the toolbox.

"Himey is finished with his bath, and Mrs. Litey's napping. Took her medication without a fuss. What I'd give to have Will visit every day."

Miranda thought the same thing.

"Leak fixed?" Nell inspected the cupboard under the sink.

"For now."

"What a dirty trick you played on that poor unsuspecting man."

"I did no such thing." Miranda pretended naïveté.

Nell chuckled as she opened the refrigerator and removed items in preparation of dinner. "We both know you could have fixed that leak easy as him. Maybe easier."

It was true. Miranda had grown up scrappy. There wasn't much she couldn't repair, be it mechanical, electrical or automotive.

"Men like feeling useful. I was merely feeding his ego."

"Right." Nell's reply dripped sarcasm. "You wanted a reason to get close to him."

"What if I did?"

Her friend and employee arranged chicken breasts in a baking pan. "Honey, if Will Dessaro hasn't succumbed to your charms by now, I doubt he ever will."

"I disagree."

"Other than he's handsome as sin, I'm not sure why you bother. There are plenty of other single men in town more than willing to walk into any trap you set."

Miranda picked up the toolbox, planning on returning it to the garage. "I feel sorry for him. He can't be happy living how he is. Alone and isolated."

Nell covered the seasoned chicken with foil and popped the pan in the oven. "And you think you're the one to draw him out?"

"Why not me? Besides, I owe him for helping me the day of the fire. It's the least I can do."

"Ah! I see. You're returning a favor."

"Exactly."

"Favor, my foot," Nell scoffed. "You like him. More than you want to admit."

Miranda headed out the kitchen door, through the laundry room and to the garage, where she set the toolbox on a crowded shelf. Nell's belly laugh trailed Miranda the entire way.

She wasn't annoyed or offended. How could she be, when Nell's assessment was spot on? She did like Will. Liked him more every time she saw him. And she wasn't about to let a little case of shyness on his part get in their way.

Chapter Two

Will didn't make it to the end of Miranda's street before his hands started to shake. By the time he reached the main street running through town, the shaking had traveled up his arms to his shoulders, making driving impossible. Luckily no one was behind him, and he waited at the stop sign.

A whine and a nudge to his arm distracted him. Cruze pressed close, instinctively sensing his master's need for comfort. Will draped an arm around the big dog's neck. Only when he could safely steer the truck without causing a wreck did he proceed onto the main road.

Up ahead, the Paydirt Saloon came into view. He turned into the lot and parked his pickup in the space farthest from the entrance. There he quit fighting and yielded to the panic, his first full-blown attack in over four years.

No matter how he tried to relax, he couldn't breathe. His lungs refused to draw in sufficient air. His heart labored to beat, hindered by the giant invisible vise squeezing it. Sweat soaked his shirt even as chills racked his body. His stomach pitched, threatening to expel the tea and cookies he'd recently consumed.

Will was going to die. Even Cruze's head resting on his leg didn't calm him.

The small part of Will's brain hanging on to reason assured him the fear was temporary and would pass. It always did. But for the next five minutes, he believed in his imminent demise.

All because Miranda Staley, with her long blond hair and laughing blue eyes, had flirted with him and had sat close enough that their legs had brushed.

Little by little, the panic subsided. Eventually Will felt nothing but stupid. He was thirty-two years old. A grown man. Not some high school junior, when he'd suffered his first attack. Back then he'd had good reason, when a tragic automobile accident had changed his life.

A pretty woman throwing herself at him, however, was nothing compared to that trauma, or the one he'd suffered when his grandmother had died. Miranda was no reason for him to lose it. Not when he'd come so far, done so well since moving to Sweetheart.

Will flipped down the sun visor and studied himself in the small mirror. The face of a stranger stared back at him. Pale, drawn, with deer-in-headlights eyes.

"I think I'm in big trouble, boy."

In reply, Cruze licked his face.

When Will had told Miranda he needed to return to the ranch, he hadn't been lying, and he had every intention of doing exactly that. But not now. The Gold Nugget was the last place he wanted to be. Too many people and too many questions. Especially with him looking the way he did.

The Paydirt Saloon was familiar ground. He stopped by two or three times a week after work for a beer. Oddly enough, a bar was a good place to seek out when a person craved solitude. The patrons understood Will wasn't the social type and respected his wish to be left alone. Routines also helped soothe him.

Pulling out his phone, he texted his boss, Sam, and let him know he'd be late, confident there wouldn't be a problem. Then he grabbed his jacket and gave Cruze a last pat before he cracked open the window and shut the door. This time of year the temperature could drop significantly the moment the sun dipped beneath the mountain peaks. The shepherd mix would rather wait for Will in the truck cab, curled up on a blanket, than be left at home alone.

Inside the bar, Will received a round of enthusiastic hellos from the twenty or so customers. After that, nothing. As luck would have it, his favorite stool at the end of the bar was unoccupied.

The middle-aged woman bartender, who also happened to be the owner of the Paydirt and the mayor of Sweetheart, was already filling a mug with his favorite brew by the time Will had settled himself on the stool, his jacket laid across his lap.

"Thanks," he muttered when the beer was slid in front of him.

"Same here." The mayor accepted the bills Will left on the bar, which covered his drink and a tip.

That was the extent of their conversation. As the minutes passed, more patrons came in, Friday-night regulars getting a head start on the weekend.

Before the fire, Sweetheart had boasted three drinking establishments. Two had burned down. While one of the other saloons was currently undergoing repairs, it wasn't yet operational, leaving the Paydirt to service the needs of the entire town and the few tourists who had recently returned.

Sitting there sipping his beer, Will remembered Sweetheart as it was before the fire. He'd worked for High Country Outfitters, taking tourists on trail rides, fishing trips and hikes in the summer, and cross-country ski excursions in the winter.

Honeymooners had made the town into what it was. Named after a pair of sweethearts who had met on a wagon train passing through the Sierra Nevada Mountains during the gold rush, the town had gained popularity around the turn of the twentieth century. Couples had eloped here in droves, thanks to a judge who had turned a blind eye when it came to verifying ages. The mayor's distant uncle, in fact.

He had retired after ten years, but the honeymooners continued to come. Hundreds of weddings were performed every year. The entire town's economy had relied on the wedding trade and—until the Gold Nugget had closed a few years ago—fans of the show *The Forty-Niners*.

Last summer, careless hikers had abandoned a still-burning campfire, which had caught and destroyed over nine thousand acres of spectacular mountain wilderness—along with the town of Sweetheart.

The honeymooners and tourists had abandoned the town. Profound devastation didn't exactly make a nice backdrop for a wedding. And tourists didn't want to hike trails or ride horses through a blackened wasteland. As a result, the town had nearly died.

Then three months ago Sam Wyler, Will's boss, had purchased the Gold Nugget and converted it into a working cattle ranch where guests could experience the cowboy way of life. Will, who'd lost his previous job in the wake of the fire, was hired on and began the newest phase in a life of many phases.

Even with the ranch, Sweetheart was slow to recover. Nearly one-third of the original thousand residents had moved away. Homeless and unemployed, they'd had no choice. Will was fortunate. His new job suited him fine, and the single-wide trailer he resided in, while not much, satisfied his needs.

"There you are."

Will turned at the deep voice addressing him, surprised yet not surprised. "Howdy."

Sam Wyler claimed the empty bar stool next to him. Will turned his attention to his half-empty beer mug. He wasn't much in the mood for company, even good company like Sam's.

"I was in town having the oil changed in the truck. Got your text and figured I'd join you." Sam signaled Mayor Dempsey for a beer.

"Sorry about not heading straight back to the ranch."

"No problem." The beer arrived and Sam took a swig. "You've worked for me, what? Three months? Four?"

"Something like that."

"If you want to take a long lunch once in a while, you won't hear me complain."

They drank in companionable silence for several minutes. Will liked Sam. More than that, he respected the man. He'd done a lot to help the town after the fire. Not only had he brought back the tourists and created jobs for a few fortunate locals, he'd helped home owners and business owners rebuild by bringing in an architect and a construction contractor.

As the hometown boy who'd returned after a nine-year absence, Sam was well liked, if not loved, by all. He'd further cemented his place in the community by marrying his former love, Annie Hennessy, last month. Theirs had been the first wedding in Sweetheart since the fire. It was also the only one so far.

The entire population was concerned about the lack of honeymooners. Especially the mayor. She and Sam had sponsored a contest for a free wedding and a week's stay at the ranch, hoping to generate publicity. In addition to a ceremony in the chapel and a honeymoon cabin at the ranch, the couple would also receive free tuxedo rentals, photographs and a fully catered reception at the Paydirt Saloon.

The winning couple was scheduled to arrive next week with their families. Everyone in town, especially the business owners, hoped and prayed they were the first of many.

Will had been assigned to the contest winners and their families, his job to make sure they enjoyed themselves at the ranch and to teach them the basics of calf roping. The last thing he needed was to be suffering from panic attacks right now.

"You okay?" Sam asked.

Will considered his answer. His boss wasn't one to stick his nose in Will's personal business. Not that a simple, "You okay?" qualified as prying.

"Fine."

"If you want to talk about what happened—"

"Nothing happened."

"If you say so. But this is the first time you've taken a long lunch."

Three more minutes of silence ticked by.

"You stop by Miranda's today?" Apparently his boss wasn't going to let this go.

"Yeah."

"Is Mrs. Litey all right?"

"Same."

Sam had known the ranch's curator from when he had spent time in Sweetheart as a younger man. For thirty years the woman had given tours of the iconic TV ranch and had overseen the daily operations. Her Alzheimer's and inability to remember Sam was hard on him.

"Then I guess it's Miranda that's bugging you."

That got Will's attention. He slanted Sam a sideways glance.

"Hey, I like the woman," Sam said. "Even if she's caused me and my contractor a pile of grief. Insisting the sheriff issue him all those tickets…"

"Not her fault her neighbor's house burned down and that the work crews are always parking their trucks in front of her place." Will's defense of Miranda came out stronger than he'd intended.

"'Course it's not her fault. And she does need unobstructed access to get those residents of hers in and out."

Will didn't respond. Instead, he focused on his breathing. Steady. Rhythmic. He didn't feel another panic attack coming on, but why take the chance?

"Ask her out," Sam said.

"What?"

"Just get it over with. Same as plunging into ice-cold water. What's the worst that could happen?"

Besides falling apart in front of her? The last woman who'd seen that happen had left him on the spot, taking his pride and heart with her. "No."

"Why not? You like her."

"She's not interested in me."

"You're wrong, pal." Sam took a long swallow of his beer, making Will wait. Finally he said, "She asked Fiona about you. And Irma."

Sam's mother-in-law, who worked as manager of guest relations at the ranch, and the housekeeper.

"When?"

"A while ago. After the fire."

That made sense and was nothing to get excited about. Miranda was probably curious about the man who'd shown up out of the blue to help her and her residents evacuate.

With no family in Sweetheart to worry about, Will had quickly gathered his few possessions, a week's supply of food and water and his dog. On a whim, he had driven to the group home on his way out of town, deciding to make sure Miranda and her residents got out safely.

Good thing he had. Corralling five frightened and confused senior citizens was no easy task. Even with Will's assistance, it had taken a while. That was the day he had first met Mrs. Litey.

While Miranda had transported her van load of residents to her parents' house in Tahoe City, Will had camped out on Grey Rock Point, an area two miles from the fire, until they had been allowed to return to their homes. It was the farthest he could venture out of town without becoming violently ill.

Sweetheart was more than his haven. In some ways it was his prison. And Will was perfectly okay with that. All his needs were met right here in town.

Food. Shelter. Employment. Companionship, such as it was. If he was sick, he went to the clinic. If he had a cavity, he waited for old Doc Bulregard's twice-monthly mobile dental visits. If he required something that wasn't readily available in Sweetheart or couldn't be shipped in by mail order, he did without.

"Then again, last week," Sam said.

Will's brows rose. "She asked about me last week, too?"

That seemed to be the reaction his boss wanted. "Yep. She's interested. And I'd say it's mutual."

"Got too much on my plate to be distracted by some gal."

"Like what? Taking care of the contest winners?"

"You said to make sure they had a great time. And there's the cross-country ski trails. This whole place will be covered in snow within a month. Maybe sooner. I need those trails marked as of yesterday."

Sam reached under his hat and scratched behind his ear. "Not sure how coffee or even dinner with a pretty gal is going to screw with your schedule."

Maybe not, but Will couldn't tell Sam the real reason. His boss, he was sure, suspected there was more amiss with Will than a craving for privacy and an aversion to conversation. They had worked closely these past months. And even if Sam had guessed Will suffered from post-traumatic stress disorder, Sam didn't know the real cause and never would.

"You don't make your move soon, pal, someone else will." Finished with his beer, Sam stood and left. He didn't ask if Will was staying or leaving.

Will stayed. He debated ordering another beer and settled on a bowl of the mayor's homemade chili and a side of corn bread. By the end of the meal, he'd reached a decision.

He wasn't going to ask Miranda out. He couldn't risk jeopardizing his job. His entire life. The contentment— if not happiness—he'd found after nearly sixteen straight years of living hell.

In fact, if possible, he wasn't going to talk to her ever again.

And the only way to accomplish that was to stop visiting the senior-care home and Mrs. Litey.

MIRANDA SAT IN the visitor's chair, her spine ramrod straight. Not an easy feat considering the cushion beneath her felt like a bed of thorns. She struggled not to squirm as the mortgage banker at the desk across from her reviewed her records.

"I haven't missed a single payment. Until this month," she amended when he peered at her from above the rims of his reading glasses.

"You were also late with your August, September and October payments."

"Yes, sir." She refused to let his brusque manner intimidate her. "The fire was unexpected. And a burden on all of us."

"Your house was spared."

"For which I'm grateful. But as I mentioned earlier, I lost one of my residents."

"Will you be replacing him?"

"There's nothing I'd like more, but Sweetheart's a small town. We're growing old folks as fast as we can."

He scowled, apparently not finding her stab at humor particularly funny.

Well, fine. Be a stiff. If she'd had a choice, she'd take her business to a different bank. Unfortunately, the modest branch of Northern Nevada Savings and Loan was the only one in town. It was also where she'd originally obtained her mortgage and hoped to refinance.

"I bring in enough money to cover my costs with the four remaining residents," she pointed out.

"*Just* enough. If I may ask, Ms. Staley, how is it you pay for your personal expenses? I assume you have some. Clothing. Health insurance. Credit cards."

Her chin lifted a notch. "I'm making do."

For about two more weeks. The plumber's fee had cut into her rainy-day fund. Will was right last Friday when he'd suggested she keep her appointment with the plumber. The leak had worsened, defying even Miranda's skills.

"If I could refinance my mortgage—" she looked hopefully at the banker "—and lower my monthly payments, I'd manage better until I took in a fifth resident."

"Which could be a while. You said yourself there aren't many 'old folks' in Sweetheart."

"I've had some recent inquiries." She was *so* going to pay for lying.

"I'm sorry to inform you, but refinancing isn't possible without being current on monthly payments and after all late fees are satisfied."

Late fees. She hated to ask how much those were. "I'll have November's payment first of the week."

"Next week is also when your December payment is due. Do you by chance have it, as well?"

She lowered her gaze. "I will, I swear."

He tapped her records into a neat rectangle and placed them in a file folder. "When that happens, we can continue this discussion."

Disappointment welled up inside and choked her. "Please, Mr. Carter…" She couldn't finish.

"Ms. Staley." He removed his glasses, and his eyes weren't unkind. "I wish I could be more accommodating.

But the bank's policies aren't negotiable. You must be current on your payments in order to refinance."

"I understand." She wouldn't cry. Not in this stuffy cubicle with the other bank employees hovering within earshot.

"There are some programs available," Mr. Carter said. "For customers in arrears. Significantly in arrears. You don't qualify yet. We can, however, check into it later."

When Miranda *was* significantly in arrears.

Not going to happen!

"Thank you for your time." She slung her purse over her arm. "I'll be in touch. Soon."

She made her way out of the bank and onto the street. Damn, damn, damn. Where was she going to get the money? Her foster parents would gladly assist. Except Miranda wouldn't ask. They'd loaned her the down payment to buy the house with the agreement she'd repay them in five years.

At the rate she was going, five years was looking more like six or seven.

Fueled by anger and frustration, she walked rather than drove the short distance to the Sweetheart Medical Clinic, where an order of medications for her residents waited. One way or another, she'd figure out a solution to her dilemma. She was nothing if not resourceful.

Halloween had only been four weekends ago, yet storefronts were already displaying Christmas decorations. Normally folks in Sweetheart pulled out all the stops, transforming the town into a winter wonderland. She didn't think the same would happen this year. Hard to be in a festive mood when most people were barely hanging on.

Her spirits sank lower when she saw a going-out-of-business banner strung atop the door of Forever and Ever Jewelry Store. Though she didn't know the owners well, she felt sorry for them. One by one, all the wedding-related businesses that had survived the fire were closing.

On the plus side, several businesses were showing hints of growth. The Rough and Ready Outdoor Depot, Dempsey's General Store and Trading Post and the Lumberjack Diner, for instance. Businesses not dependent on the wedding trade.

Maybe the mayor was wrong. Instead of trying to lure back the honeymooners, what if they concentrated on the tourists? Those wanting to experience cowboy life at the Gold Nugget Ranch, mountaineers and skiers and even amateur prospectors.

Only how would that help her? Honeymooners or tourists, it made no difference to the number of elderly citizens requiring supervised care.

At the clinic, Miranda was asked to wait until a staff member was available to review the medications with her. A young girl sat at a miniature table, coloring in a book. Her mother paid no attention, glued instead to whatever was displayed on her phone. The girl smiled tentatively when Miranda winked at her.

Someday Miranda would have children of her own. A houseful, like her foster parents. And like her foster parents, she didn't care if the children were biological or products of the system. Both, hopefully. She was a pay-it-forward kind of person.

"Miranda," the nurse called out. "Your order's ready."

She was just turning to leave when the door leading to the examination rooms opened and Will stepped out. She noticed his surprised expression first, then the splint encasing his left wrist.

Grabbing the sack of meds off the counter, she rushed toward him. "Are you all right? What happened?"

"It's nothing."

She pointed at the splint. "That's not nothing."

"I had a small run-in."

"With what? A two-ton tank?"

"A calf." He started toward the exit.

She followed him, refusing to be put off. "A calf broke your wrist?"

"Sprained it."

Honestly his clipped answers were sometimes quite annoying. "How, for crying out loud?"

"It pinned me. Against the fence."

She gave him a pointed stare. "What shape is the calf in?"

One corner of his mouth lifted ever so slightly. "This round went to him."

Miranda was transfixed, like the other day in her kitchen. Only then, a flash of heat in his eyes had been responsible.

"Mr. Dessaro?" the nurse called right before they reached the door. "You forgot your pain medication."

"Don't need it."

"You say that now," Miranda cautioned. "Wait till tonight."

He shook his head.

"Trust me. I'm a nurse. Don't try to be tough. A sprain is painful. You're going to want some relief. About ten o'clock tonight you'll be crying like a baby."

After a moment's hesitation he returned to the counter and paid for his medication. The small white bag containing his prescription promptly disappeared inside his jacket pocket.

She waited for him by the entrance. He insisted on opening the door for her with his good arm despite her protests.

Miranda suppressed an eye roll. *Men.*

A chilly breeze swept along the sidewalk, engulfing them and forcing them to take momentary shelter beneath the clinic awning. She snuggled deeper in her wool coat. "Won't be long now till the first snow."

"Yeah." He touched the brim of his cowboy hat. "See you."

"Hold on a sec!" She had absolutely no reason to keep him from his next destination. Yet she couldn't stop herself. "You haven't dropped by to see Mrs. Litey since Friday."

"Been busy."

"She misses you."

"How is she doing?"

"Obliging part of the day. Cantankerous the rest. If you could spare a few minutes, I know she'd love to see you."

Oh, sweet Lord, Miranda should be ashamed of herself. Using poor old Mrs. Litey to manipulate Will for purely selfish reasons.

"Can't."

"Tomorrow, then?"

"We'll see."

His *we'll see* had the ring of *not likely.* "Did something happen? I mean, other than your sprained wrist?"

"No."

Hmm. She didn't quite believe him. "I know this is a ridiculous suggestion, considering the weather, but would you want to have an ice-cream sundae with me?"

She'd clearly rendered him speechless, not that it was hard. After several false starts, he uttered, "Thanks, but no—"

"Please," she said, cutting him off. "I've had a really crummy afternoon, and I could use some high-calorie, high-fat comfort food. Along with an ear to bend. I promise you won't have to contribute much to the conversation. I'll carry it all. I'd invite you for a beer," she blurted out when she sensed a refusal forthcoming, "but you can't have alcohol with your pain meds."

Just when she had decided her efforts were in vain, he muttered, "Sure," under his breath.

Miranda smiled for the first time that afternoon.

Chapter Three

The ice-cream parlor, across the street and up half a block, had recently reopened after sustaining significant damage in the fire. Miranda liked the remodeling job, though the place lacked the ambiance of the old one.

A few of the original furnishings had been salvaged, including a pair of wrought-iron chairs with heart-shaped backs from the fifties, glass root-beer mugs from the sixties and a Coca-Cola poster the owner swore was his great-great-aunt's from the roaring twenties.

All the spared items were currently stored and on display in the brand-new Sweetheart Memorial Museum. Annie Wyler, Will's boss's new wife, had donated the land—on which her family's inn had once stood—to the memorial and paid for its construction out of the insurance settlement money. It was a grand gesture and much appreciated by the folks of Sweetheart.

Miranda had been by the memorial three times so far. She particularly enjoyed seeing what new items had been donated, most of them stirring happy memories of her childhood from age seven on, when she'd come to live with her foster parents.

Before age seven had been less happy. Miserable, actually. She didn't forget those days, either. Miranda accepted the cards life dealt her, learned from them and moved on. What else was a person to do?

Sneaking a glimpse at Will sitting across from her in the booth, she supposed there were other options. One could hang on to the past. Retreat into it. Let it disempower them. In her opinion Will had done all those things.

She took another spoonful of her brownie delight hot-fudge sundae and almost groaned in ecstasy. "How's your…" What was it he'd ordered? "Scoop of plain vanilla ice cream?" She failed to mask her disdain.

"It's okay."

"You should have ordered a little hot fudge with that." She relished an even larger spoonful of her sundae.

"Maybe."

"Seriously, Will, what does it take to wring more than one or two words out of you?"

He observed her from over his spoon. The small glint of heat she'd seen the other day in her kitchen reappeared, lighting eyes as dark as the hot fudge that had been generously poured over her ice cream.

Proximity. To her. That was what it took to wring more words from him. Well, she could certainly arrange for proximity. Lots of it.

"What went wrong?"

"I beg your pardon?" She dabbed at her mouth before melted ice cream dribbled down her chin.

"You said you had a crummy morning."

"Oh, yes. That." For a brief second she lost her appetite. Fortunately it returned, and she dug into her remaining sundae. "My appointment at the bank didn't go well."

"Your appointment?"

"I'm trying, hoping, to refinance my house. Problem is I've had a little trouble making the monthly payments on time since losing a resident." Miranda didn't wave her dirty laundry in public. But she was also a plainspoken person, and Will had asked.

"The bank won't cut you any slack?"

"No. Rules are rules and policies are policies. I can possibly refinance if I bring my account current."

"How far behind are you?"

It was a rather bold question for someone who rarely spoke. "Two months as of next week. Then, when I make November's payment, which I will on Tuesday, I'll only be behind one month."

"What are you going to do?"

She sighed and set down her spoon. "Whatever I have to. I'm not losing my house or my business. I have worked too long and hard to get it off the ground. My residents need me. I'm the only certified elder-care facility in Sweetheart run by a registered nurse. If I go under, they'll have nowhere to live."

All right, she was being melodramatic. Other than Mrs. Litey, all her residents had family to go to.

"Any prospects?"

"No. Not at the moment." She didn't fib to Will as she had to the banker.

"You can't go under."

No, she couldn't. Will stating as much piqued her interest. Did he care? For her or Mrs. Litey?

"Thanks for the support. If you by chance have a relative needing supervised care hiding in your back pocket, I have a room available."

"I wish I did."

His sincerity touched her. Without thinking, she reached across the table and laid her hand atop his uninjured one. For several seconds he froze. Then he jerked his hand away with such speed, he knocked her arm sideways.

Miranda gathered herself, feeling a little hurt. "Sorry about that. I'm a touchy-feely kind of person. Goes with the territory, being in the medical profession and from a large family."

He remained silent.

"Look, Will, I didn't mean to upset you."

She noticed then that he was breathing regularly. Really regularly. As if he was counting his breaths. His hands had disappeared beneath the tabletop, and she thought she heard the snapping of a rubber band against skin.

Well, wasn't that curious?

She wanted to ask him about the snapping—who wouldn't?—but, for once, she curbed her impulses. What she'd learned about Will during the past few months was that he defined the term "private person" and wouldn't appreciate her prodding.

"I didn't… I wasn't expecting it."

She hadn't been expecting it, either. Reaching for Will's hand had been an impulse. The response to a moment of feeling connected to him. She'd thought—hoped—the connection was reciprocal.

"Hey, no worries." She grabbed her spoon and polished off the last of her sundae. "I'm not easily offended. If I was, I wouldn't surround myself with crotchety old people and a smart-mouthed aide."

"Are they really that bad?"

"Other than Mrs. Litey? Heavens, no. I love my job. I even love her. On her good days."

The reminder that he hadn't been around much wasn't lost on him. "Give her my best," he said with an end-of-discussion abruptness.

As if that would stop her. "Which is it? Your work or visiting Mrs. Litey?"

Now it was his turn to ask, "I beg your pardon?"

"What don't you want to talk about?"

He developed an avid interest in finishing his boring single scoop of vanilla ice cream.

"Fine. None of my business." Except she wasn't able to keep her mouth shut. "The thing is, I've come to depend on your visits, and I shouldn't have. Mrs. Litey is my responsibility."

"I like visiting her."

"So it's work, then."

"I've been marking the cross-country ski trails."

"How's that going?"

"Not easy."

"I imagine the fire's made it hard to find decent trails."

He nodded.

"If you need any help, give me a holler." When his brows lifted in surprise, she said, "What? I know these woods better than most. Better than you, I bet."

"Right."

"Ha. You forget, or maybe you don't know, my dad was assistant superintendent of the Sierra Consolidated Mining Company. He dragged us kids over every inch of these mountains when we were growing up."

"Your mother's also a nurse."

Well, well. He'd done some of his own research. On her. Miranda was pleased.

"I followed in her footsteps. After earning my degree, I worked a few years at the Renown Regional Medical Center in Reno. That's where I became interested in elder care. When I moved back to Sweetheart, I worked at the clinic with my mom for a while. Then the economy tanked, and Dad lost his job at the mining company. He and Mom moved to Tahoe City. She still works as a nurse, and Dad's a stay-at-home Mr. Mom. I have two new foster sisters, nine-year-old twins."

"How many altogether?"

"Foster siblings? Eight. And my parents love every one of us like their own. They're pretty amazing people."

"I'd say."

"What about your parents? Are they in the Tahoe area?"

"No."

"Another state?"

"No."

His short replies were no doubt intended to put her off, but they only served to make her more curious. Will was a puzzle, and Miranda had a fondness for puzzles. "I take it you aren't close to them."

He waited a beat before answering. "They're dead. They were killed in an accident."

She nearly jumped at the jolt that shot through her, and pressed a hand to her middle. The sundae in her stomach sat like a heavy stone.

"I'm so sorry." She couldn't imagine the horror of losing both her parents at once. "How awful for you."

He looked at her across the table, emotion once again flaring in his eyes. Not heat and definitely not passion. Anger perhaps? Remorse?

"It was more awful for them," he ground out.

"When did it happen? How old were you?"

Standing, he announced, "I have to go," and let in a gust of cold air as he exited the parlor, which reached Miranda clear on her side of the room. She waited a minute before collecting her things.

Will was even more complex than she'd originally thought. And more damaged. She'd be smart to leave him be, as he clearly wasn't ready for any kind of romantic relationship.

Except Miranda didn't think she could. She wasn't just attracted to him or challenged by him, she was fond of him. Growing fonder by the day. He was like no man she'd ever met.

Outside she glanced up and down the street. Her car was parked two blocks away, near the bank. Seeing the building's brick facade, she was again reminded of her financial dilemma. Determination surged inside her. She wasn't one to let a minor setback derail her from her goals. If she needed extra money to keep her business afloat, she'd get it. One way or the other.

Setting off, she strode confidently toward the Paydirt Saloon. During college when she'd come home for the summers, she'd worked part-time at the Paydirt, earning extra money to supplement her scholarships.

The mayor was clearing tables amid the sparse gathering of afternoon regulars. Behind the bar, the mayor's son washed glassware. Both issued her a friendly hello.

"What can I get you today?" the mayor asked when Miranda approached.

Without hesitating, she relieved the mayor of the tray she was holding and reached for the towel on the table. "A job. Even a few hours a week if that's all you have."

Mayor Dempsey studied her critically.

Miranda braced herself for a slew of questions. Why did she need a job? What about her elder-care home? What made Miranda think there was a position available when employment in Sweetheart was as scarce as crow's teeth? She also braced herself for rejection.

To her overwhelming relief, the mayor's expression softened. "I assume you can start today."

"You able to ride with that bum wrist?" Sam asked.

Will tugged the cinch tighter and looped the excess strap into a tight knot. Gripping the pommel and back of the seat, he tugged and demonstrated how little his injury bothered him by testing the saddle's stability.

Rocket Dog, a stout, sassy four-year-old mare that had originally belonged to Will's former employer, High Country Outfitters, pawed the ground in anticipation. This one liked the cold weather and the challenge of climbing steep frost-covered hills. She was a perfect match for Will's current mood.

"Why aren't you taking one of the ATVs?" Sam leaned against the corral fence and crossed his arms over his chest.

Will double-checked the maps in his saddlebags and his supplies. Two bottles of water, a thermos of black coffee and a protein bar. That should be enough to last the morning.

"Some of the trails I want to mark are blocked by fallen timber."

Easier to ride a horse over the obstructions than drive an ATV around them. In his opinion anyway.

"I'm thinking you have enough trails already marked. We don't have many skiers making reservations."

"Could change."

He wasn't one to oppose his boss, and if Sam insisted, he'd cancel the outing or take an ATV. In truth, the ride was more for him than work related. Will needed the solitude and the feel of a horse beneath him. The more he was in the company of others, the more tangled his thoughts became. Alone he could sort them out and compartmentalize them. Less likely to plague him that way.

Why had he told Miranda his parents had died? No one in Sweetheart knew that about him. Not even Sam.

For the past two days, his and Miranda's conversation in the ice-cream parlor had replayed over and over in his mind, affecting his every waking moment. All he could see was her eating that damn sundae and him revealing the darkest of many dark moments from his past.

"Don't forget a poncho," Sam advised.

Both men glanced at the sky. Clouds had been gathering since dawn. They weren't yet heavy with snow, but weather this time of year was unreliable at best.

"Got one."

"The contest winners and their families are arriving to-morrow afternoon. I'd like to introduce you to them once they're registered and settled into their cabins. Over dinner. The following morning you can give them a tour of the ranch."

"Sure."

The dining hall wasn't scheduled for construction until spring. In the meantime, guests were served family-style meals in the kitchen of the main house. Hearty country breakfasts every morning comprised the usual fare, with the occasional dinner. Like tomorrow, in honor of their special guests. Most people seemed to enjoy sitting at the same table as the cast members of the show *The Forty-Niners* once had.

Will's presence at a meal had only been requested once before. When his boss had gotten married.

He and his bride had looked happy that day. Sometimes when Sam didn't think anyone was watching, he wore the same dopey smile he had during the ceremony. With their two daughters from their respective previous marriages, they were now one big happy family.

Will envied his boss. Happiness like that had once been within his reach.

Lexie had been his first love and the woman he believed he'd spend the rest of his live with. But then, he'd also believed he'd conquered his PTSD. He'd been wrong on both counts and had learned a very hard lesson. Women didn't want a broken man.

"I only ask because I'm wondering how long you intend to stay in the mountains."

Will slanted Sam a look.

"Bedroll. Tarp. Rope." One by one, Sam listed the items Will had packed.

"Two hours. Three at the most."

"Okay. Just making sure. You've been burying yourself in work the last couple of days. Not that you don't always bury yourself in work."

"It's important the winning couple have a good time."

"Yeah, but the entire burden of their stay doesn't rest on your shoulders."

Will retied the bedroll behind his saddle and patted the mare's rump, a signal to Sam that he was ready to leave.

"How's Mrs. Litey?"

"Don't know."

"When was the last time you saw her?"

Apparently Sam wasn't ready to cut Will loose yet. "A while."

"Is there a reason you're avoiding her?"

"I'm not."

"Miranda, then."

"I better head out while the weather's holding." Will didn't wait for a response. He flung the reins over Rocket Dog's neck and mounted her in one fluid move. Cruze jumped up from where he'd been lying and waiting.

"Sorry, boy. You need to stay here."

The shepherd mix instantly planted his hind end on the ground. He used to hate being left behind. Lately his age had started to show, and a trip to town would exhaust him. He'd be there when Will returned, or in the barn.

"Do me a favor, will you?" Sam patted Cruze's head, letting Will know his dog would be watched during his absence. "On your way back."

"Sure." As long as it wasn't stopping by a certain elder-care group home.

"Mayor Dempsey has a package for me. Some vouchers for the contest winners. Can you pick them up at the Paydirt on your way back?"

"Will do."

Will didn't normally ride through town, though he had before. During Sweetheart's early days and up until *The Forty-Niners* had ceased production, horses were a common sight on the streets.

Saluting Sam, Will turned Rocket Dog toward the long

tree-lined drive leading from the ranch. Halfway to the main road, he chose a partially hidden trail, one used more by deer and elk than humans. He and Rocket Dog were immediately engulfed by towering ponderosa pines.

Will was in his element. He rode the mare hard, down one hill and up the next, until their breathing was labored. The terrain, still thick and green despite the encroaching winter, didn't last. Within a mile, the forest gave way to a sea of barren, blackened land. This was how close the fire had gotten to the Gold Nugget.

Skirting the border of the vast wasteland, Will stopped occasionally to dismount and mark the trail with a red plastic tie fastened to a low-slung branch. Only the most stalwart and athletic of riders, hikers and cross-country skiers would choose this trail. He couldn't wait to lead them.

At one point he nudged Rocket Dog across a rushing stream. Well, more like a babbling creek until spring, when the snow melted. Then crossing would be tricky. At the very top of the hill, where the stream originated from an underground spring, Sweetheart's original settlers had chanced upon gold and had staked a claim. They'd prospected the area for thirty years until it had panned out.

Will thought the old claim, with its discarded and derelict equipment still there, might make an interesting rest stop and noted it on his map.

Hard riding and fresh air took his mind off Miranda, but only for a short while. Too soon, he was back to thinking about her. Constantly.

Had she and her father visited this mining site when she was young? Did they hike this same path? Picnic at this same spot along the creek? View the town nestled in the valley below from this same vantage point? Why did she waste even a minute of her time with him?

Will couldn't fathom the answer.

Two hours later, the narrow trail merged with a larger

and more frequently used one that led to town. By now the mare's steps were slower, her excess energy having been spent. Will relaxed and let her set the pace for the last leg of their trip. Miranda still filled his thoughts, but caused him less anxiety.

In his opinion, the woods surrounding Sweetheart showed no signs of recovery from the fire—other than the forest service's clearing the network of dirt roads. Scorched pine tree trunks stood at bent angles, resembling an army of ghoulish stick soldiers. Here and there a tree remained, miraculously spared from destruction. It would be years before the seeds from their cones produced new generations.

Will wondered if winter, with its gray skies and heavy blankets of snow, would be kind and hide the forest's blemishes, or unkind and magnify them.

His ride down Matrimony Lane drew a lot of stares and a few waves, which Will returned with a nod. He didn't admit to searching every female face for Miranda's. At the Paydirt Saloon, he tethered Rocket Dog to the old hitching post beside the building. Drooping her head, she eagerly indulged in a well-deserved snooze.

Inside, the mayor hailed Will from behind the bar and reached for a clean mug. "The usual?"

"Not today."

"What brings you by?"

"Sam sent me. You have some vouchers for him."

She frowned in confusion. "What vouchers?"

"For the contest winners."

"Don't know what he's talking about."

"I'll call him." Will reached into his jacket pocket for his cell phone and dialed Sam. His boss didn't pick up. "Must be a mistake."

"Try again in a few minutes. In the meantime, have a beer."

"How 'bout a water?" He wasn't in the mood for drinking.

Finding his regular stool open, he sat and attempted to reach Sam again, with the same results. Disconnecting, he debated what to do.

"You look as if you are wrestling with a mighty problem."

At the sound of Miranda's voice, he sat instantly straighter.

"We know it's not Mrs. Litey, unless you're feeling bad about ignoring her. She misses you something awful, by the way."

Will suffered a stab of remorse.

"You shouldn't make her pay just because you're mad at me."

Having no choice, he turned slowly around. "I'm not mad at you."

"Seems like it." She stood with a serving tray propped on her hip, a red apron tied around her waist and a pert scowl on her pretty face.

He blinked in disbelief. "You're working here?"

"Part-time." She squared her shoulders. "Just until I catch up on the mortgage payments. So I guess we'll be running into each other, seeing as you're here a lot."

He suppressed a groan. His one place of practically guaranteed solitude had just been invaded.

It was in that moment that he realized there were no vouchers and never had been. His boss knew about Miranda's job and had set Will up.

The snake.

"Well, what'll it be, cowboy? Can't rent that bar stool for free." Miranda flashed him a saucy smile that sent his pulse rate into the triple digits. "Swiss-and-bacon burger's on special today."

She moved closer—on purpose, he was sure of it—until

her thigh brushed his knee. He swallowed hard and waited for the panic attack, ready to bolt at the first sign.

To his shock, it didn't come. And when he spoke, his voice sounded normal.

"I'll take mine medium well."

Chapter Four

Miranda made sure there was just the right amount of sway to her hips as she walked away from Will. Not so much as to be obvious and not so little as to be overlooked.

He noticed the sway. No reason to turn her head, she could feel his eyes boring into her.

Will might be shy as a choirboy with his first crush, but he was all man.

"One Swiss and bacon, medium well." She passed the order ticket through the window to the cook in the kitchen.

Mayor Dempsey hailed her over to the bar. Opening two longnecks, she tipped her head at Will. "You going to put him out of his misery anytime soon or just keep torturing him?"

"What are you talking about?"

She lowered her voice. "He's not the kind you toy with, Miranda. That heart of his has been through the wringer. Anyone can see it."

"I don't toy."

"You don't exactly handle with care, either."

She delivered the longnecks to a far table where a pair of truckers sat. They would be gone in the morning, having off-loaded their cargo of kitchen cabinets to the Abrams, one of many local families in the process of rebuilding their homes.

"Thank you," she said cheerily when they dropped a tip of several singles on her tray.

They definitely took note of her swaying hips. And as a glance across the room confirmed, Will took note of *them*.

Okay, maybe she did toy with him a little.

She couldn't help herself. He liked her, it was obvious. Desired her, even. Yet there he sat, watching, but not running after her as other men had. Not even *walking*. She was determined to get him up and moving in her direction.

Fancy that. Miranda Staley doing the chasing for once, rather than the other way around.

"Hey, Miranda, bring us another round, would ya, darling?"

"Right away, Henry."

The cattle rancher's table wasn't far from Will. She made a point of passing right by him when she delivered the drinks to Henry and his cronies.

Will's gaze stuck to her like superglue. Miranda felt her cheeks redden. Seriously! When did a man ever make her blush?

Apparently now.

The mayor's words came rushing back to her: *that heart of his has been through the wringer.*

Sweet, darling man. To have lost his parents. How old had he been? she wondered. Not that it made a difference. Losing them at any age would be tragic.

Miranda had no idea if her own birth parents were alive or not. She tried to care. Tried to muster an ounce of compassion and affection for them. A shred of curiosity as to their whereabouts. But any feelings she might have had for them were lost when they'd abandoned her for three whole days in an old car because they were too high to remember they even had a daughter.

Losing her foster parents, however, was an entirely dif-

ferent matter. Miranda ached at the mere thought. Nothing
would leave a larger, emptier hole in her life.

Would she withdraw the way Will had? Avoid relationships? For a while, certainly. For years? It was hard to say.
Miranda was resilient. More than that, her foster parents
wouldn't want her to close herself off. They were gregari-
ous, affectionate people who had taught their children to
live life to the fullest.

"Order up," the cook called.

Saying hi to her newly arrived coworker, Cissy, Miranda
collected Will's Swiss-and-bacon burger from the window.

"Here you go." She scooted close to Will, setting the
generously laden plate down in front of him. "Enjoy."

He gazed hungrily…at her. Not at the plate of food. Miranda flushed again.

This was just plain silly, she silently chided herself as
she went about clearing a recently vacated table. When
Cissy emerged from the back, tying her apron, Miranda
tried to distract herself by making small talk. It worked
only until she caught Cissy giving Will a decidedly preda-
tory once-over.

"I've been trying to get his attention for ages," she confessed out of the side of her mouth when they met up at the
bar to collect fresh drink orders.

"Any luck?" Miranda wasn't normally the jealous type.
She could, she realized, become that way. Cissy was certainly attractive, in a flashy sort of way. Maybe Will preferred that over Miranda's country-girl looks.

"Don't I wish," Cissy sighed.

Miranda busied herself refilling salt and pepper shakers
before the dinner crowd arrived in full force.

"He's sure noticing you," Cissy said.

Miranda glanced quickly at Will and pretended non-
chalance. "Oh?"

"As if you didn't know."

"We're friends. He comes by my elder-care home. To visit one of my residents," she clarified.

"Uh-huh." Cissy's reply oozed sarcasm.

"No, really." If Will had been wanting to visit Miranda all along, he wouldn't have recently stopped.

"Well, I'm giving you fair warning. If he decides to be *my* friend, I'm totally taking him up on it."

Hmm. Like hell.

The saloon was filling up by the minute and she was running around like crazy. Even so, Will was never out of her visual range for long. More than once their glances connected.

She tried reading what lay behind his expression without success, which only served to increase her interest. When he pushed to his feet and reached for his hat on the bar, she was right there beside him.

"You leaving?"

"I have to get back before dark."

"It's only five."

"I'm riding."

"You are?"

She'd missed seeing him arrive by horseback. She wouldn't miss seeing him leave. Will astride a horse was a worthy sight.

"Later." He touched the brim of his hat.

"Does that mean you're stopping by the house soon?"

"I'll try." At least his tone was more positive than the last time.

Donning his jacket, Will left, zigzagging between the tables, his long strides taking him to the door in a matter of seconds.

Without thinking, Miranda set down her tray on the end of the bar and announced to Cissy, "I'm on break. Be back in ten," then hurried after Will.

"Hey!" the other server called out.

She kept going, ignoring the twinge of guilt pricking at her. She'd make it up to Cissy later.

Will beat her through the door and was halfway around the side of the building by the time she burst outside.

Holy, schmoley, it was cold! She should have remembered her coat. Well, there was no going back now.

Hugging herself, she ducked around the building and came upon Will checking the cinch on his saddle before mounting. The horse bobbed its head in eager anticipation.

Miranda wasted no time. "Will!"

He turned, surprise registering on his face. "I left the money for my tab on the bar."

"It's not that."

"What then?"

She started to shiver, from nerves as much as the cold. Clearly she should have thought this plan through a little more, come up with an excuse for waylaying him. And remembered her coat.

Her shivering increased until she was shaking. "P-p-please come visit Mrs. L-L-Litey."

"You're freezing." He took a step toward her.

"For h-her sake. N-n-not mine."

"Dammit, Miranda."

The distance separating them disappeared. In the next instant he was wrapping her in his arms and drawing her against his chest. It felt nice. He rubbed her arms, creating a soothing friction. She burrowed deeper, and a sound of contentment slipped out before she could stop herself. His arms tightened their hold.

She waited. Surely he would kiss her. When he didn't, Miranda raised her face to his.

Nothing.

She parted her lips and linked an arm around his neck, inching even closer. Still nothing.

Really? Okay, the guy might be shy, but he wasn't dense.

He could be wearing a gunnysack over his head and not realize she wanted him to kiss her.

More drastic measures were clearly called for.

"Will?" She rose on tiptoe, their mouths close enough she could feel his warm breath on her skin.

"Yeah?"

"I'm not cold anymore."

"That's good."

The horse nickered impatiently, but Miranda paid no heed. Her other arm joined her first as she anchored herself more securely to Will. "In fact, I'm quite comfortable."

He immediately stiffened and started to pull away.

As if she would let that happen. "Dammit, Will. Enough with the game playing. Kiss me already."

"You don't understand."

"You're right. I don't. But that's no reason to stop." Releasing an exasperated breath, she angled her head and planted her lips firmly on his.

The earth didn't move, bells didn't ring and fireworks didn't explode. Miranda might as well have been kissing the back of her own hand.

Wasn't that a disappointment.

Honestly, how could she have been so mistaken? The kind of heat she'd seen lighting his eyes usually hid a blazing fire.

No sense making a fool of herself any longer. She started to peel herself off him—only something held her in place and refused to let her go.

That something was Will's arm, locking itself firmly across the small of her back.

"What are—" She didn't have the chance to finish whatever random thought had popped into her head.

Will's mouth came down on hers, hot, hungry and all business. She let him take control, not that she had much of a choice, and found she didn't mind in the least. He knew what he was doing.

Sweet angels in heaven, what had possessed her to think the man couldn't kiss?

The earth moved, bells rang and fireworks exploded all at once, leaving Miranda light-headed. The sensation intensified when Will pushed her up against the hitching post. The hard surface kneading her back was ignored as the entire length of his body met and covered the entire length of hers.

When his hand came up to cup the side of her face, she increased her hold on him, fusing their mouths even more firmly together. The resulting sizzle and sparks were off the charts. Miranda couldn't recall ever being kissed with such fervor. She rather liked it and wanted him to go on and on.

Only he didn't. To her disappointment, Will released her. Frigid air instantly invaded her every pore, the chill even more noticeable after having been encased in the warm cocoon of his arms.

"Sorry," he muttered.

"Why?" She grinned. "I liked it, in case you didn't notice."

He stared at her, his gaze devouring.

Miranda melted beneath it. Reaching for his cheek, she let her fingers trace the line of his bristled jaw. "We can go for round two, if you have a mind to."

Something in his expression changed. Before she could ask what was wrong, he pivoted and stepped into the stirrup. Swinging his leg over the saddle, he pointed the horse in the direction of the street and nudged it into a brisk trot.

"Goodbye," she called after him, but he didn't acknowledge her. Dammit, had she scared him away? It wouldn't surprise her.

Miranda followed him as far as the street, watching him

ride away as dusk quietly fell. She didn't move for several minutes, despite the freezing temperature.

That, she realized, was how it felt to be thoroughly kissed. And by Will Dessaro, of all people. Who'd have guessed?

WILL MANAGED TO stall his panic attack until he reached the outskirts of town. Then all his coping techniques proved worthless. It was his worst attack in years. Since the "Dear John" email he'd received from his ex-fiancée while stationed at Fort Huachuca in Arizona.

Giving Rocket Dog her head, he let the mare carry him home. She didn't seem bothered by his shaking, cold sweats and hyperventilating. When he could take no more, he bent forward over the saddle horn and waited for his heart to stop drilling a tunnel through his rib cage.

He'd kissed Miranda. Kissed her like a crazed man. He would have done it again if not for getting the hell out of there when he did.

What would she think if she saw him now, on the verge of passing out? Worse, what if the panic attack had struck while their lips were locked?

She wouldn't have wanted a round two. She wouldn't want him anywhere near her house, either, Mrs. Litey or no Mrs. Litey.

Eventually the attack receded. Though he didn't feel like his old self, he regained enough control to maintain a semblance of normalcy. Taking stock of his surroundings, he fumbled for the reins.

Rocket Dog was dutifully retracing her steps along the route they'd taken into town through the mountains. Will changed direction, opting for a quicker route that would have them home in a third of the time. He needed coffee. Better yet, a shot of whiskey. Anything, as long as it hit his stomach with the fiery jolt he craved.

He'd kissed Miranda. His muddled brain had yet to fully process the shocking revelation. His body, however, recalled every moment in precise detail. The taste of her lips. The extraordinary sensation of her generous breasts pressed against his chest. Her tiny moan of pleasure when he'd backed her into the hitching post. Each memory reminded him of how many years it had been since he'd held a woman.

She was everything he'd imagined. More than he'd hoped for. When she had first touched her lips to his, he'd been convinced he could hold out by not moving a muscle. Then his resolve had snapped and he'd practically manhandled her.

Except she'd said she liked kissing him. Had clung to him as if she couldn't get enough. It may have been a long time for Will, but he could tell when a response was genuine.

No more and never again, he told himself. This was his one and only slip. He wouldn't screw up his life, not after all the progress he'd made. Even for Miranda.

Rocket Dog's rhythmic clip-clopping on the hard-packed dirt road worked like a mantra and further calmed Will. By the time they passed through the Gold Nugget's main gate, it was well after dark and he felt good enough to fool anyone he came in contact with. Except for Sam.

As luck would have it, his boss was waiting for him at the horse corrals, standing in a pool of light cast by the flood lamp mounted overhead.

"There was no envelope," Will announced, and dismounted. Snowflakes were just starting to fall, melting the instant they landed.

"No? I swear Mayor Dempsey told me she had one." The smirk Sam wore erased any doubts Will might have been entertaining about a ruse. "Run into anyone interesting?"

"Why ask when you already know?"

Sam didn't miss a beat. "Speaking of someone interesting, we have a visitor waiting to talk to you."

Will raised his brows.

"Meet us in the kitchen when you're done unsaddling." Without elaborating, Sam took off across the large yard and toward the ranch house.

Despite his resolve not to, Will hurried, oddly anxious about the mysterious visitor. It was too early for it to be the contest winners—they weren't due to arrive till tomorrow afternoon. Carrying the saddle and bridle into the tack shed, he brushed down Rocket Dog in record time and put her up for the night. Then he made his way to the house.

His boots hit heavy on the wooden steps. Wicker rockers flanked both sides of the entrance, inviting guests to sit and enjoy the panoramic view, as did a porch swing. Someone had hung a giant wreath, complete with a red bow, on the front door. Probably Sam's wife. It gave a homey look to the place and reminded Will of his grandmother's house.

The smell of something delicious invaded his nostrils the second he entered the house. Sam's mother-in-law, who also worked for him, was an exceptional cook. She must have fixed dinner for them before leaving at the end of her shift. Too bad Will had already eaten.

"Hey, Cliff," he said upon spotting the guest sitting at the kitchen table.

"Will, how are you doing?" Cliff Dempsey was the mayor's nephew and local sheriff. He wore his uniform, which gave Will reason to suspect the visit was official.

Sam motioned for Will to sit. "Did you eat at the Paydirt?"

He nodded. "But I wouldn't mind some dessert."

While the other two men served themselves hearty portions of chicken casserole and salad with homemade Thousand Island dressing, Will carved out a large slice of blueberry pie—his favorite.

Small talk filled the spaces between bites of food. Will was acquainted with the sheriff—most folks were. He was also aware that his boss's friendship with Cliff went back a lot of years. More years than Will had been in Sweetheart.

He had the undeniable impression he was being set up a second time today and waited for the purpose of the meeting to be revealed. The moment came at the end of the meal over coffee. Thankfully it was strong and black.

"Cliff and I have been talking." Sam inclined his head in the direction of the sheriff. It was apparently a cue for Cliff to take the lead.

"As you know, we have a volunteer fire department in town. Such as it is."

Will did know. The crew of a dozen men had fought valiantly last summer when the fire had swept through Sweetheart. They'd been limited by their minimal ranks and one dilapidated fire truck from the Stone Age.

"The town council met last week and voted to expand the department," Cliff continued. "That includes newer modern equipment and additional personnel."

Here it came, thought Will, a request to volunteer. It wasn't the first time he'd been targeted for recruitment. He'd declined then, too. Not because he couldn't perform the work or that it didn't appeal to him. It did. Very much.

What held him back was his fear of having a panic attack in the middle of a call. He was generally good in a crisis, demonstrating his ability often during his six years in the army. But those had been the easy years when his attacks were under control. He'd hate for someone to be depending on him for their life or the protection of their property, only to fail them.

"Sounds good." He kept his tone noncommittal.

"You're on our short list of candidates."

Before he could squeeze out a reply, Cliff plowed ahead. "The council also voted for one paid position. One that, given recent events, they feel is essential. We want the tourists coming here to feel safe. Our residents, too."

Will waited, something he was good at and tried to envision what this new position had to do with him. Search and rescue, perhaps? Made sense, given his army experience. He'd decline that, too. For the same reasons.

"An EMT," Sam interjected, clearly losing patience. "You."

"Me?" Startled, Will drew back. "I'm no EMT."

"Not yet." Cliff chased his last bite of pie with his last swallow of coffee. "The town will pay for your training. You'd have to spend two full days a week in Reno. The council secretary has all the info on the school and is ready to enroll you. Your gas and hotel would also be covered as part of the deal."

Reno! Impossible. Will hadn't left Sweetheart once in the five years since his arrival.

"All the council asks for in return is three consecutive years of service, starting immediately after you graduate. Which, I think, is more than fair."

"It's a great opportunity, Will," Sam said.

"And you'd be paid for being on call," Cliff added. "Whether or not there was an emergency."

"You'd have to stick nearby on your days off at the ranch." Sam shoved his plate aside. "That's one downside."

In Will's opinion, it was the only selling point.

He felt a familiar constriction in his chest. With both men observing him, he couldn't reach under the table and snap the rubber band he wore. Instead he focused on his breathing and murmured, "I can't. I have no experience."

"You're more than qualified." Cliff leaned forward, consciously, or subconsciously, pressuring Will. "Weren't you an orderly in the army?"

"For a while."

Two years. And during that time, he'd been in love.

Deeply. And believed he'd be married by the next spring when his and his fiancée's respective enlistments were up. But that didn't happen, and the attacks returned, every bit as severe as after his parents had died.

"An orderly isn't the same as an EMT," he said.

"Which is why you'd attend school." Cliff clearly didn't see a problem.

Neither did Sam. "If you're worried about your job, don't be."

Will couldn't look at his boss.

"I'll pay your wages on the days you're at school."

He jumped on the convenient excuse. "I can't take your charity."

"It's not charity. I'm making a donation to the town."

Sam had received a huge settlement two years ago when his first wife had unexpectedly died in a car crash. After returning to Sweetheart, he'd sunk a good portion of that settlement into revitalizing the town, wanting to use the money for good and give meaning to his late wife's tragic demise.

"If I'm not earning the money by working, it's charity," Will insisted.

"We can argue that point," Cliff interjected. "But what I'd rather do is focus on the needs of the town and the pool of potential candidates. You're a good fit, Will. You're young, strong, athletic and levelheaded in a crisis."

Little did they know.

"We've seen you in action." Sam picked up where Cliff left off. "Not just with Miranda Staley's residents during the evacuation, but last year when that hiker went missing. You found him at the bottom of the ravine on Grey Rock Point, splinted his broken ankle and hauled him out of there in one piece, strapped to your back."

"You also rescued my uncle from his car when it careened into a snowbank," Cliff said. "Middle of winter.

He might have died from hypothermia if not for your efforts. You have what it takes. What we're looking for. What we need."

Will didn't disagree. And if he were a different person, burdened with a different affliction, he'd seize the opportunity with both hands.

"I can't," he repeated. The last time he'd tried to leave Sweetheart, he'd heaved all over his boots.

"Take a few days," Cliff said, "and think about it. Get back to me when you're ready." He stood and carried his dishes from the table to the sink. "In the meantime, there are a dozen reports to review and a stack of phone messages calling my name."

Sam accompanied Cliff to the front door. Will stayed where he was, listening to the sound of their voices until the words were too low for him to decipher. They were probably scratching their heads, trying to account for his lack of enthusiasm.

It *was* a great opportunity. The only time he felt good about himself, other than on the back of a horse, was when he helped people. Particularly those in a crisis. He couldn't make amends for failing to save his parents when he'd had the chance. But in his mind, his actions in those moments honored their memory. Much like Sam spending his late wife's insurance settlement for the good of the town.

If only he could…

Forget it. Impossible.

Long before Sam returned to the kitchen, Will escaped out the back door to his pickup truck parked next to the barn and, ten minutes later, to his single-wide trailer.

Spending a restless evening pacing back and forth in front of Cruze's watchful eyes, he finally fell asleep, only to dream about being an EMT. And in his dream he was free from anxiety, free from fear, free from the guilt that constantly ate at him and able to love again.

Miranda's face was the first thing he saw when Cruze's whines jarred him awake just as dawn was breaking.

Chapter Five

"Whoa there, Trevor!" Will grabbed the boy's arm a split second before disaster struck. "Guests aren't allowed in the livestock pens."

Will knew the boy's name because his older cousin/babysitter had called it out—along with his sibling's name, Demi—at least twenty times in the past twenty minutes. The pair, niece and nephew of the bride, were tornadoes on wheels, getting into everything and listening to no one.

"Why not?" Trevor demanded in a belligerent tone Will had begun to suspect was permanent. "They're just calves."

"Calves can be dangerous."

"How?" Demi demanded. She didn't want to be left out. "They're just baby cows."

"Baby cows that can kick and butt and stomp. You might get hurt."

"No calf's gonna kick me." Trevor stabbed his narrow chest with his thumb.

"You think?" Will held up his still-bandaged left wrist. "See that? A calf pinned me. Against the fence."

The kids' eyes went wide. "Did you break it?" Demi asked.

"A sprain. Could've been worse."

"Did it hurt?"

"You bet. I couldn't write for a week."

Trevor grinned, displaying overly large front teeth his

face had yet to grow into. "Cool! I want to get pinned by a calf. Then I won't have to do my homework."

"Not on my watch, you won't."

"What does that mean?" Demi asked, obviously more curious than her brother.

"Not while I'm in charge of you," he explained.

The pair followed him to where four of the ranch's tamest horses stood tied to the arena railing, saddled, bridled and ready to be ridden. Trevor pestered Will nonstop, which he attempted to take in stride. Will generally liked children and related to them better than he did adults, with the exception of the elderly, like Mrs. Litey. Trevor and Demi, however, were more taxing than most youngsters their age, and he had to remind himself frequently to relax.

All hope of that was lost when they were joined by the cousin/babysitter, Cora, a nineteen-year-old college student who flirted outrageously with Will at every opportunity. With each flash of her dimples, toss of her hair and accidental-on-purpose bumping into him, his defenses rose.

It was all for a good cause, he reminded himself. Everyone in Sweetheart would benefit from the couple's wedding. According to the mayor, news crews from Reno were arriving soon to cover the ceremony and the touching story behind the town's attempt to recover from the fire. Will would do his part.

After a tour of the ranch earlier that morning, the couple and their immediate family members had taken a trip into town, where they were meeting with the mayor at the Paydirt about the reception and with the Yeungs at the wedding chapel about the service.

The remaining family members had been left in Will's care. In addition to Trevor, Demi and Cora, the group included a teenaged girl who refused to look up from her cell phone even when she and Will were introduced. At least she didn't try his patience.

Their activity of choice was calf roping, and he'd been instructed by Sam to give them lessons. Since their experience was limited to pony rides at the fair, Will was starting with the basics: Horsemanship 101. Later, they'd progress to lariats and roping dummies. If their attention lasted that long. He had his doubts.

Cora managed to finally pry the teenager loose from her phone, convincing her to pocket the device while they were on horseback. She sent Will a didn't-I-do-good head tilt.

He nodded in return. When it came time for her to mount, she needed more assistance than the kids, maneuvering Will into holding her by the waist and hoisting her into the saddle.

Once seated, she gushed, "Thank you," and lifted the reins. "How do these thingies work?"

He wrapped her fingers around the "thingies." Then said, "I'll show you. In the arena."

"And here I was hoping for some private instruction."

He pretended not to understand. "Only group lessons are available."

Mounting Rocket Dog, he aimed the mare toward the gate. The cousin/babysitter followed him into the arena.

As if he would be interested in her. For starters, she was much too young for him. And though she probably turned the head of every guy on campus, Will was thinking of only one woman these days. Miranda Staley had invaded him completely. She was in his head, under his skin and, he was afraid, had wormed her way into his heart.

Why her? Why now? Just when everything was going well. First there was the fire, then her. If he hadn't driven by her house during the evacuation, he wouldn't now be distracted, edgy and ready to jump at the slightest provocation. His four young charges weren't helping the situation.

As it turned out, the phone-toting teenager was the most

natural and talented rider in the bunch. Apparently she loved animals.

Will checked the sun, noting its very slow trek across the sky, and expelled a tired breath. He didn't own a watch, but Miranda did. A sleek, sporty number that was both stylish and practical.

A lot like the woman herself.

Where was she now? he wondered. At the group home or the Paydirt, helping the mayor serve lunch to the winning couple and their entourage? What about her house? If she didn't refinance, she might lose it, and her residents depended on her.

"You okay?"

Will glanced up. The cousin/babysitter had stopped trotting in circles to stare at him.

"Fine."

"You look as if you have a lot on your mind."

Miranda had made a similar remark to him not long ago. He'd been thinking of her then, too.

"Guess I do." He made a quick visual sweep of the arena. The two youngsters and the teenager happily walked or trotted their mounts.

"I have a lot on my mind, also." Cora arched her brows, striving for allure. "I'd love to get out of here and cozy up in front of the fireplace."

Will wanted out of there, as well. Only not for the same reasons. But he'd sworn off visiting Miranda's house.

While he was attempting to devise an excuse to escape Cora, Trevor suddenly kicked his horse in the sides and yelled, "Giddyap!"

The horse—a fat, lazy swayback—broke out in a slow, slow trot.

"Giddyap," Trevor yelled again and continued kicking the horse.

Will nudged Rocket Dog into a lope and rode up beside

the boy, cutting him off and forcing him to stop. "That's enough."

"Why won't she gallop?"

"Because she's smarter than you and knows you aren't ready for that."

"We are, too, ready," Demi insisted. She'd gotten her horse to trot as well, and reined to a stop beside them.

"After a few more lessons, maybe."

Trevor frowned and jerked too hard on the reins. "I wanna rope a calf."

"You treat that horse better," Will said firmly, "and we'll see about roping."

The boy looked startled, then chagrined, and not at all used to being reprimanded.

"If you're going to be a real cowboy, you have to take good care of your horse. He's how you make your living." Will stroked Rocket Dog's neck. "There might come a day when he saves your life."

"You made that up."

"I didn't. Ask any of the hands here at the ranch. Ask Mr. Wyler. He got lost up on Cohea Ridge once. Rode all night in circles. Too tired to care, he gave the horse his head. They were home by breakfast."

Trevor's gaze narrowed. "Did that really happen?"

"True story." It was easier to tell the kids about Sam than his own recent ride back to the ranch during a panic attack. Without Rocket Dog, he might have wound up as lost as Sam.

The tale of Sam's harrowing escapade quieted the boy for a while, and they finished the riding lesson without any more incidents. Will still thought of Miranda—when didn't he?—but kept his mental forays better hidden.

When it came time for learning to rope, Will tied the horses to the arena fence. The ground was the best place to start. Almost immediately the teenager lost interest. Pulling out her cell phone, she walked silently away, immersing herself in a game or texting.

Cora also lost interest after her multiple attempts had failed to entice Will to wrap his arms around her and demonstrate the proper way to hold a lariat. "I have to get back to the cabin. Come on, kids."

"Not yet," Trevor complained.

"We're having fun," Demi seconded.

"Then stay." The cousin/babysitter flounced off, but not before flipping her hair one last time.

Will considered sending the kids with her and then decided, what the heck? The pair were enjoying themselves and behaving reasonably well for a change, not caring that their ropes missed the practice dummy far more than they connected. Resting a forearm on the arena railing, he breathed easy for the first time all morning.

"Seems to be going well." Sam had arrived when Will wasn't looking.

He shot Cruze a dirty look. What good was a watchdog that didn't bark? "Well enough."

Sam nodded in the direction of the kids. "Ran into their older cousin. She raved about you. Said she's going on the afternoon trail ride."

Will was suddenly not looking forward to the rest of his workday.

Sam studied him. "Something happen I should know about?"

"Nothing."

What was there worth mentioning? That the gal had flirted with Will, and he'd been indifferent? Knowing Sam, he'd be far more interested in the reason for Will's indifference. He'd pin the blame on Miranda and Will's attraction to her. Sam would also be right, to a degree. Although Will's ex-fiancée had also done her fair share of damage long ago.

"Have you thought any more about the town's offer?" Sam asked.

Evidently Will's respite was at an end. He should have figured as much when Sam had shown up unannounced. Deprive Will of the opportunity to prepare.

The tension coursing through Will intensified. "You just asked me two nights ago."

"You've had more time to consider."

"My answer's the same."

"Classes don't start until the second week of February. Take your time."

"Put your weight on your right foot," Will called to Trevor. When the boy's rope landed closer to the plastic calf head, Will asked, "Feel the difference?"

Trevor whooped with delight at his accomplishment. Demi tried, missed, scowled and tried again, doing better than Trevor. She also whooped and delivered a victory punch in the arm to her brother.

"About the offer—"

"More time won't change my mind."

"The town needs you," Sam went on, pitching the job to Will with skill that would shame a telephone solicitor.

Will's chest slowly compressed as if someone were pushing a fist into his sternum, and the skin across his face felt tight as heat flooded his cheeks.

Not now. He closed his eyes. *Not in front of Sam.*

Guilt. It was triggering another panic attack. The therapists, all three that he'd counseled with over the years, had warned him about the dangers of getting into situations similar to the one that had started the attacks at sixteen.

Fear of disappointing people. Of not being there when they needed him. Of letting them die when he might have saved them.

Only through sheer concentration was he able to bring the panic attack under control.

"More time might not change your mind, but you're going to get it. We're willing to wait." Sam didn't stop there. "What about the volunteer fire department? Can we count on you? Training starts soon."

"Where does it take place?"

"Does it matter?"

"Kind of." *Breathe. Relax. Stay calm.*

Sam gazed quizzically at Will. "Here at the ranch. And at the West 47 Forest Station. In the mountains near Grey Rock Point and the test fire sites we've selected."

Will could possibly handle that. And if he agreed to serve as a volunteer firefighter, Sam might lay off him about becoming an EMT.

Then again, he might pressure Will even more. But as a volunteer firefighter, he'd be part of a team. That was why he'd done so well at the hospital.

"Maybe."

"Great." Sam clapped Will on the back. "I'll tell Cliff."

"That wasn't a yes."

"Close enough to one."

Will was in a losing battle, so he changed the subject. "Did the wedding party return from town yet?"

"About twenty minutes ago."

"Come on, Trevor, Demi," he hollered. "Quitting time."

"You can't get out of it that easy." Sam sent him an incriminating look.

"The lesson's over."

"Don't think you can stop caring about people by avoiding them. Not grow attached to a place by staying away. Trust me. That's not how it works. I tried for nine years, then came back to Sweetheart and Annie."

His was probably right, but Will was going to try anyway.

"I get it," Sam said. "Something happened to you. Something you don't want to talk about. But if you ever feel the need, I'm available."

Of everyone Will was acquainted with, Sam would be his first choice for a confidant. When he was ready. Should that day ever come.

"Thanks."

Sam nodded briskly and left, disappearing into the barn. Will appreciated what his boss hadn't said more than what he had.

Trevor stomped over to retrieve his rope from the practice dummy, his sneakers smacking the hard ground. "Aw, do I have to?"

Will half expected the boy to throw a tantrum. He didn't. Will went to him and patted him on the head. "Good job."

Demi hugged Will around the waist. "Can we do this again tomorrow?"

"If your parents say it's okay." Will had a full schedule, but he'd find the time.

It was easy for him to show affection to these two. They were leaving soon, making them emotionally safe. Same as the guests he took on trail rides. He could be friendly, generous and even open. All because he wouldn't see them again.

He'd see the folks of Sweetheart again. And if he suffered a panic attack during an emergency call that resulted in a loss or death, he'd have to face them over and over, knowing what they thought of him. Feeling their disappointment. He couldn't live with that, and leaving would be his only option.

Run away. As he always did. Miranda had pegged him to a T.

One more reason he wasn't the man for her.

After showing the kids where and how to stow their lariats, Will escorted them to their family's guest cabin. He had about two hours to kill before Doc Murry, the local vet, arrived to treat a horse with an infected tooth. Will could head to his trailer and grab a leisurely lunch. There were also plenty of chores around the ranch needing doing, and he didn't mind the overtime.

Don't think you can stop caring about people by avoiding them. Not grow attached to a place by staying away. Trust me. That's not how it works.

Sam was right. Will hadn't and couldn't stop caring no matter how hard he tried.

The proof came five minutes later when his cell phone rang. He didn't recognize the number, but the voice that responded to his hello was unmistakable.

"Hi, Arthur."

"Will, I hate to impose, but is there any chance you can come by the house? It's Leonora."

Mrs. Litey? "Is something wrong?"

"She's having a fit. Worse than usual. Miranda isn't here and Nell can't handle her. Which is saying a lot as that woman could milk a rattlesnake with one hand while flipping pancakes with the other."

Against his better judgment, Will said, "I'll be right there," and took off to let Luiz, the head ranch hand, know he'd be back soon.

At least he hoped he would.

MIRANDA OPENED THE door. Will stood there, the startled expression he wore every time he saw her firmly in place. "I didn't expect to see you here today," he said.

That made two of them. She leaned against the doorjamb and assessed him critically. "This *is* my house."

"What I meant was…" He winced guiltily. "Arthur said you were at the Paydirt."

She put him out of his misery and retreated from the doorway, letting him inside. A large tree stand blocked his path. "Watch your step. Himey almost took a header earlier. I've had to banish him, Mr. Lexington and Crackers to the kitchen. Nell's keeping guard."

"This is some obstacle course."

Will maneuvered around and over the dozens of boxes containing Christmas decorations spread throughout the room, many with their colorful contents spilling onto the floor. Christmas had officially arrived at Harmony House.

"I blame my parents," she clarified. "With so many different children from so many different cultural and religious backgrounds, we grew up celebrating every December holiday."

The decorations also gave the place a pleasing, homey appearance and cheered Miranda. Her residents, too. Except, apparently, for Mrs. Litey.

"Arthur confessed that he called you." Though Miranda wouldn't dare admit it, she was secretly glad. She and Will hadn't spoken since their kiss the other day, and she was fairly certain he'd been avoiding her.

"He sounded desperate."

"And you were at the Paydirt," Arthur said, coming to his own defense. He and Babs were stationed in front of the TV. Miranda had insisted the volume be kept at a reasonable level.

"I got off early. Business was slow." She took both Will's hat and sheepskin-lined jacket. "These will be on the coatrack when you're ready to leave. And, as for you, Arthur..." She wagged a finger at him, purely for show.

He shrugged in apology, his hand, as always, firmly clasping Babs's. "No one can calm Leonora like Will."

"How is she?" Will asked.

"Being exceptionally contrary today." Miranda released a tired sigh. "She refuses to let me or Nell clean her room, won't touch even the tiniest morsel of food and refuses to take her medication. There's a large slice of rhubarb pie with your name on it if you can convince her to cooperate."

"I'll try."

"Crackers!" Nell called from the kitchen. "Get back here."

The terrier was quicker than the caretaker. He bolted into the front room and straight for Will, who bent and scratched the dog behind the ears, calling him a good boy.

Why couldn't he greet Miranda with the same affection? Not scratch her ears, but a warm glance would be nice. They'd locked lips after all, and pretty heatedly. Surely that warranted an intimate exchange.

Miranda suppressed a shiver of excitement just recalling the feel and taste of him. She'd especially enjoyed the way he had assumed control, covering her body with his as he had pushed her into the hitching post. If only she could get him alone today.

Next to impossible with a houseful of people.

"We heard the contest winners arrived at the ranch and are making their way through town." Arthur was clearly attempting to divert her attention away from himself.

He had no need to worry. Will had already done that by simply standing there.

"Yes, sir," he said.

"Bet things are hopping at the ranch."

"I love the Gold Nugget." Babs leaned forward in her wheelchair. "Haven't been there in ages."

"I'll take you." Arthur's smile was besotted.

They were simply adorable. Truth be told, Miranda was kind of jealous.

"Me, go to the ranch?" Babs patted the armrest of her wheelchair. "In this contraption?"

"Miranda will drive us." Arthur's glance was filled with hope.

Not a bad idea, she thought. "We'll see."

"Will can give us a tour."

"Name the day," he responded agreeably.

Did he realize she would be there, too?

"I thought maybe I scared you off for good," she said when they were finally alone and walking down the hall.

"Almost."

Was that a joke? He was so damned hard to read sometimes. She snuck a peek at him from beneath lowered lashes and decided no. The set of that exquisite mouth was much too serious.

"Surprise, Mrs. Litey. You have a visitor." Miranda moved aside so that the older woman could see Will from where she sat in her chair.

Her face, frozen with displeasure since the moment she'd awoke that morning, brightened. "Joseph! You're back." Struggling to her feet, she hurried to him and threw her arms around his neck. "I'm so glad to see you."

"Mom." He enveloped her in a tender hug and patted her thinning white hair.

Tears welled in Miranda's eyes and she blinked them away. Really, she was such a sap.

But who could blame her? Will possessed a heart of gold, even if he tried to hide it. For elderly women with Alzheimer's anyway.

"Perhaps you're hungry," Miranda said, hoping he remembered that Mrs. Litey hadn't eaten all day.

"Yeah, I am. What about you, Mom?"

"Of course you want to eat. You must be starving after that long drive. Were the roads bad? It's been snowing." The elderly woman's gaze darted to and fro, confusion enveloping her like a thick fog. "I haven't been to this restaurant before. Perhaps we need to look at a menu. Miss, can you bring us some menus, please?" she appealed to Miranda. "And two glasses of ice water."

"I'll be right back." Before leaving, Miranda paused and motioned to Will. From behind the shield of her hand, she pointed to the nightstand and the small paper cup containing Mrs. Litey's pills. Sitting beside them was a glass of juice.

He nodded in understanding.

She made a beeline for the kitchen, relief coursing through her. Mrs. Litey had the ability to shake up the entire household, making it hard on everyone. The days were rough, the evenings nearly impossible. The slightest thing could set her off. Miranda found herself biting her lip more than once during Mrs. Litey's "sundowning" episodes—which had decreased in frequency since Will had started visiting her but not ccascd.

"From the sounds of it, you've got company." Nell abandoned stirring a pot of stew on the stove when Miranda entered the kitchen.

"Not me, Mrs. Litey."

"Right." Nell drew the word out over several beats.

"Right," Himey repeated, copying Nell's grin. "We all know that young man is here to see you." He was sitting at the table, shuffling a deck of cards but not playing.

Miranda wished Will was here to see her. "Her Highness would like menus. I think she'll be okay if I just bring food. Something simple."

"I have leftover tuna from lunch yesterday." Nell opened the refrigerator door. "She likes tuna."

"Remember she thinks they're in a restaurant."

"I'll cut the sandwiches into quarters. Fancy up the plates and add that broccoli salad."

"May I have a sandwich, too?" Himey pestered Nell endlessly as she prepared the light meal.

Miranda busied herself checking email on her phone. When Nell was finished, Miranda carried the tray to Mrs. Litey's room, mentally counting her blessings. What would she do without Nell?

Without Will.

The scene that greeted Miranda elicited a wave of relief.

Mrs. Litey and Will sat in the chairs, conversing quietly. The paper cup containing the pills was empty, a dip of his head confirming they'd been taken.

Miranda set the tray on the small table between them. "Here you go." She divvied up the plates, napkins and plastic tableware.

When Will took his, their fingers brushed. He instantly pulled back.

Miranda would have none of that, and made sure their fingers brushed again. Will visibly tensed, and she congratulated herself. He would not get off that easy.

"Thank you, miss," Mrs. Litey said, sweet as molasses. "I love tuna fish."

"You're welcome. Just holler if you need anything else."

Miranda didn't let it bother her that Mrs. Litey had no idea who she was. It happened all the time. To family members, as well. Mrs. Litey's brother, Reverend Donahue, a retired minister living in Carson City, called weekly. She rarely recognized him and insisted on knowing who the stranger was who kept pestering her.

Miranda felt sorry for the man. The poignant conversations he had with her afterward always tugged at her heartstrings. He loved his sister dearly and would do anything he could for her.

Returning to the task of converting the house into a holiday wonderland, she cleared the side table beneath the picture window. In place of knickknacks, she set up a musical Christmas village. Skating figurines and lit miniature streetlamps were always a hit with the residents and guests. Arthur and Babs volunteered suggestions from across the room. Miranda only half listened.

Arthur's daily visits didn't bother her, although she often thought, as much as he was here and as often as she fed him, she should charge him a fee. Then she'd look at him and Babs together and her resolve would fly out the window. They were so fond of each other. She couldn't deny Babs this one pleasure in a life that was otherwise filled with hardships.

Watching them reminded her of Will. What didn't remind her of him? Regardless of how long his visit with Mrs. Litey lasted and how quickly he needed to return to the ranch, she was going to delay him for a chat. They couldn't continue ignoring the kiss.

While deliberating how best to corner him—a piece of pie might do the trick—she accidentally dropped a tiny dog figurine. It fell behind the side table. Great. Crackers would root out the figurine and chew it to pieces.

Dropping to her hands and knees, she swept her hand over the braided rug. Where the heck was the figurine?

"What happened?" Arthur asked.

"Missing dog. No worries, I'll find it."

"Need help?" Will posed the question, not Arthur.

Startled, Miranda sat up, lowering her hind end she'd been waving in the air mere seconds earlier.

"Um…" Maybe she should forgo the chat.

"She dropped a dog." Was Arthur ever quiet?

Will's eyes widened.

"A dog figurine," Miranda clarified.

"Find it?"

"Not yet."

"Give the girl some help, why don't you?" Arthur's suggestion smacked of meddling.

Babs giggled like a schoolgirl.

Miranda wanted to bury her face in the crook of her arm. This couldn't go any worse.

To her dismay, Will joined her on the floor. With his much longer arm, he reached beneath the side table to where the rug met the wall. She was on the verge of telling him not to bother when he straightened, the dog figurine scissored in his fingers.

She held out her palm and he placed the dog in it. Their fingers brushed again. On purpose. This time, Will was responsible.

Her insides fluttered.

"Mrs. Litey's resting," he said, his voice low and appealing. "In her chair."

They were so close. Mere inches apart. Miranda watched in fascination as a small muscle in his jaw jumped. Was he nervous?

"She got sleepy after we ate."

"I should check on her."

"I think she's okay in the chair for a while."

Good, because Miranda was quite content to remain right where she was. "Thank you for your help. With Mrs. Litey and this." She set the dog figurine atop a pile of fake snow, next to a little boy pulling a red sled.

Will climbed nimbly to his feet and extended a hand. She hesitated only a second before taking it, noting again the calluses of a working man. How would it feel to have those working man's hands skimming over her bare shoulders? Down the length of her spine?

When he drew her to a standing position, their eyes met. His were guarded. Hers probably revealed far too much.

"We have to talk," she blurted out.

His eyes went from guarded to wary. "Not now."

"Will."

"Talk to the girl," Arthur insisted.

Miranda suppressed a groan. Will was already shy enough. The last thing he needed was an audience. Yet when would she have another chance?

"We can't pretend…"

"Yes, we can." He turned on his boot heels and, snatching his hat and jacket from the coatrack, strode out the front door.

Miranda remained rooted in place, torn between annoyance and frustration, much too stubborn to chase after him a second time.

Chapter Six

Nell balanced her fists on her plump hips. "What's wrong with you? Go after him."

"The man's impossible."

Miranda had retreated to the kitchen to lick her wounds after Will had left. She'd been there less than a second when Nell butted her nose into what was none of her business. Served Miranda right for residing in a house bursting with people.

"He's also getting away." Nell opened the dishwasher and began unloading it. "You want to have that chat with him, you'd best hurry."

Miranda hesitated only briefly before taking the advice. Grabbing her jacket off the kitchen chair, she shoved her arms through the sleeves. "Be right back."

"That's my girl."

She caught up with Will at his truck. He was just sliding behind the steering wheel. His dog stuck his head out the open passenger window and yipped hello. Miranda scurried to the driver's side of the truck, praying Will wouldn't start the engine.

He didn't. Neither did he close his door. She hung on to it, hope surging inside her.

"Don't go."

"It was a mistake," he ground out.

"I couldn't agree more." Her breath came quickly. "You should accept the town's offer and train to be an EMT."

His brows slammed together, shouting his displeasure louder than any words. He probably thought she'd been referring to their kiss. She sort of had—at first.

"Mayor Dempsey told me this morning that you turned them down."

The creases deepened.

"I realize you might consider the topic personal…"

He shrugged as if he didn't.

"Regardless, it is personal. In my opinion, the mayor mentioned it because she thought I might be able to influence you."

"Influence me?" That clearly surprised him. And bothered him. Enough that he reached for the door handle.

She wedged herself between him and the door. "Not because of the kiss. She doesn't know. No one does. Unless you told them."

"I *didn't.*"

"Right." She pulled the flaps of her jacket together, refusing to let his adamant denial hurt her more than she already was. "It's not as if you talk much at all. Which, I guess, is part of the problem. Hard to have a relationship with someone who doesn't communicate."

"We don't have a relationship."

"Oh, yes, we do, Will. After that kiss, you can't deny we've got something going. And there could be a whole lot more *going* if you weren't so stubborn."

"I'm not seeing you."

"Why? Because of your anxiety issues?" She almost chuckled at his startled reaction. "Don't freak out. I worked in a hospital. I specialize in elder care. I've seen patients with all types of anxiety disorders. Yours, I think, is the post-traumatic stress kind."

His eyes widened, confirming her suspicions.

"I'm not sure what caused it. Your parents' death, the army, maybe. But you're obviously struggling."

"My condition is under control," he answered tersely.

"Then why did you run off the other night? That wasn't the reaction of a man controlling his PTSD."

"This topic *is* personal." He jammed the key in the ignition and then removed it when the door alarm began dinging.

"Yes, it is, and I'm interfering. But you need to know, your PTSD makes no difference to me. I like you. Just as you are, quirks and all. I think you like me, too. And Lord knows I have my share of quirks."

"It makes a difference to me." He again reached for the door.

She didn't budge and sent him a reproving look. "Is this how you deal with all your problems? By running away?"

"I have to get back to work."

"Such a convenient excuse." She exhaled wearily, secretly surprised he hadn't left yet. "You didn't come to Sweetheart because of a job with High Country Outfitters. You were escaping. And you've been escaping ever since. What are you afraid of, Will?"

Oh, did that hit a nerve.

"I should have kept my damn mouth shut." This time when he jammed the key in the ignition, he turned it. The engine roared to life.

What had she expected? That he'd admit he cared for her and take her in his arms for a repeat of the previous night? Hardly.

With little choice, she backed away. On the sidewalk, she paused to watch him drive off. The mailman took Will's vacated spot and popped out of the truck, a stack of mail in his hand and a Santa hat on his head.

"Morning, Miranda. Have a registered letter for you."

"Thanks." She automatically signed the return slip without looking at the sender, her mind stuck on Will and their disagreement. Maybe she should have left well enough alone.

No doubt about it. But he'd become too comfortable in his isolation and could use someone breaching the defenses he had so rigorously held in place.

Only when she was making her trek up the front walkway did she start sifting through the mail. Spotting the registered letter from Northern Nevada Savings and Loan, she tore it open and came up short.

Each sentence she read caused her heart to pump faster. By the end of the letter, she was shaking. The total payments and accumulated late fees due staggered her. At the front door, she pressed the letter to her chest and mentally calculated her income over the next and past few days.

Including yesterday's tips and her first paycheck from the Paydirt, she could cover one full mortgage payment and the late fees. God willing, that would be enough to satisfy the savings and loan company. For three days. Until her grace period for December's payment was up.

Other than Mrs. Litey's mood swing from dour to docile, Miranda's day was nose-diving and couldn't possibly get worse. One step at a time, she told herself, as her cell phone started ringing. She'd forgotten it was in her jacket pocket.

Recognizing Mr. Lexington's son's number, she pulled herself together and answered with a bright, "Hello, Miranda Staley speaking."

"Miranda, hey. It's Gary. Hope I haven't caught you at a bad time."

"Not at all. Did you want to speak to your dad?" Miranda had a landline for the house, but sometimes family and friends of the residents called on her cell.

"Actually, no." There was a long pause before he continued. "It's you I want to speak with."

The seriousness of his tone unnerved her as much as the

letter from the savings and loan company had. "Is something wrong?"

"We, my brothers and I, are concerned about Dad."

"How so? He's doing great." Miranda respected her residents' privacy and waited outside the front door. It was her practice to never discuss them in the vicinity of others on the chance she was overheard.

"That's what he tells us," Gary said. "And we know he loves everyone at Harmony House. Especially you. But we miss him."

Mr. Lexington was a lifelong resident of Sweetheart. His three sons had each moved away decades ago. When the time came that he needed assistance, he'd chosen to remain rather than impose on them.

"Why don't we arrange for an extended visit? A week. Two weeks. You're only a couple hours away."

"That's an idea. Another is to…move him. My brother Sal and I both have room, what with the kids all gone."

Miranda's stomach dropped to her knees. "H-he's happy here."

"Which is why we're not rushing the decision."

Thank heavens.

"But we are seriously considering it and wanted to put you on notice. In case there are any…changes you want to implement."

Such as renting out his father's room?

Miranda had been wrong. Her day not only could get worse, it had. By leaps and bounds. "I don't think your dad wants to move."

"No. And he can be very stubborn. If we decide to go ahead with this, we'd like your help and support."

Help and support? How could she give that when it would plummet her into financial ruin? "Of course, I'll make the transition as easy as possible." The words were flat. Like Miranda's morale. "When might you be making a decision?" Her contract required a minimum notice of thirty days.

"By the end of next week. Of course, we'll pay you for the full month."

The rest of what Gary said was drowned out by the roaring in Miranda's ears. She was barely squeaking by with four residents. No way could she survive past January with just three. Even if she included her part-time wages from the Paydirt Saloon.

She had to hope that Gary and his siblings would reconsider or that Mr. Lexington dug in his heels and refused to leave. Though limited physically, he was sound of mind and still in charge of his own decisions. Miranda had learned the hard way, however, that family members could—and often did—exercise a great deal of influence.

"Keep me posted," was the most she could choke out before issuing a polite goodbye.

Tears pricked her eyes. She didn't try to stem them. Miranda was a crier. And she was a laugher and a smiler and a bit of a grouch if she was feeling out of sorts.

It was her personality. She didn't hold her emotions in check. Unlike Will, who excelled at it. Honestly they couldn't be more opposite.

She had to stop thinking about him. After the phone call with Mr. Lexington's son and the letter from the savings and loan, she had far more pressing problems to address.

Wiping her eyes, she went inside—and was immediately met by a gathering of her residents, including Mrs. Litey, out from her room for a change. Nell acted as their spokesperson.

"We were talking while you were outside," she said. "Been a while since we've had any kind of an outing."

Before Miranda could respond with a resounding no, she just wasn't in the mood, Mr. Lexington boomed, "We want to go to the Gold Nugget. See all the changes."

"Hmm. You don't say." She tapped her chin with her index finger.

If that was what he wanted, who was she to say no? Especially when his contentment might be the only thing standing between her and losing her home and business.

"EASY GIRL," WILL crooned.

Rocket Dog flinched and attempted to pull her hoof away. She didn't want anyone messing with the soft underside. A possible injury had left her even more sensitive.

Anchoring the heavy hoof more firmly on his bent knee, Will told the mare, "Something's caught in there," as if she could understand him. Maybe she did, because she relaxed. Marginally.

Using the pointed end of the pick, he dug around in the narrow area between the metal shoe and her hoof. Rocket Dog had been limping since yesterday, and Will was determined to discover the cause. The next instant, the pick struck a solid object. The instant after that, Will dislodged a pebble and sent it sailing to the ground. Rocket Dog snorted lustily.

"That wasn't so bad."

She shook her rangy head as if to disagree.

Will inspected the rest of the hoof, satisfied he'd found the only culprit. Hard to believe something so small could cause such pain, and yet it had. He could sympathize. He'd squeezed his pain into a compact ball and had been carrying it around for years.

"We have a group arriving shortly for a tour of the ranch."

At the sound of Sam's voice from behind, Will dropped Rocket Dog's hoof and straightened. "That so?"

"They'll be here at one."

Will had assumed the afternoon was his to catch up on work around the barn and corrals. The winning couple's wedding ceremony was scheduled for two and their family and friends had left for town hours earlier, including Will's newest sidekicks, Trevor and Demi. The Gold Nugget looked like a ghost town.

Bad for business, easy on the nerves, Will thought selfishly. The two days since his quarrel with Miranda had been hard on him, and he craved solitude.

"Where are they from?" Not the ranch. Will knew darn well no new guests were scheduled to arrive until next week.

"They're locals."

His curiosity was roused, but he didn't ask. Sam would tell him in due time. "Thought you and Annie were headed to the wedding."

"We are."

Will leaned back on his heels and leveled his boss with a you're-not-wearing-that look.

Sam tugged self-consciously on the hem of his Carhartt jacket. "I'm changing first. Annie and the girls have been hogging the bathroom all day."

"Hmm."

"Consider yourself lucky that you don't have to share your trailer with anyone."

Will recalled his family's comfortable suburban home where he had spent his childhood and most of his teenage years. Before a blowout in the left front tire had sent their vehicle careening off the road and into a gully. His next memories were of his grandmother's farm, with the big rambling house he'd grown to love almost as much as the cattle she'd raised and the horses she'd kept.

He would give anything to see that place again, to wander the hundred-plus acres. He'd rarely left the farm, completing his last semester of high school on campus only after a year of homeschooling and intense psychotherapy. At his grandmother's insistence, he'd attended the nearby community college. The week following his graduation, she'd dropped dead.

Her sudden and fatal heart attack wasn't his fault, yet he had been plunged into the same emotional abyss as when his parents had died. Another year of therapy pulled him out of that slump. It was his counselor's suggestion that he leave Kansas and strike out on his own.

The army might seem to be an odd choice for someone with PTSD, but it had turned out to be Will's salvation. The routine, the structure, the companionship, the environment, completely different from what he was used to, quelled the triggers that brought on his attacks. When he had met Lexie and fallen in love for the first time, he had thought his demons were completely exiled.

Stupid and naive of him. Fate wasn't done making him pay for being the sole survivor of that car crash. One day, an incident at the hospital had been too reminiscent of the car crash, and his demons had been unleashed again. Lexie had looked at him as if he were a stranger, then bolted, never to be seen or heard from again save that final, gut-wrenching email.

Instead of admitting to Sam how profoundly he missed his loved ones and what he'd give to return to those days, Will muttered, "Don't lie, you like being overrun by women."

"It has its moments." Sam's dour expression didn't fool Will. Given the opportunity, his boss would gladly add to his family and made no secret of it. "You should give togetherness a chance."

Will would if he could. But that came with a price: letting people get close to him.

A part of him envied Miranda and missed his visits to Harmony House. Granted, the place was occupied by elderly, cantankerous and demanding seniors. It was also cozy and warm and full of good feelings. Just the same as both the homes Will had grown up in.

"You're a lucky guy," was all he said to Sam.

"Tell me about it." The man's pleasure was almost contagious. "By the way, have you thought any more about the town's offer?"

"Don't you have a wedding to attend?"

"I can spare a minute to talk about this."

"My answer hasn't changed." Will propped an arm on Rocket Dog's hindquarters. She shifted to accommodate the extra weight. "I like this job just fine."

"I make it my practice not to pry into people's private business—"

"Could've fooled me."

Sam wasn't put off. "Something's bothering you. If you need help, even if it's just an ear to bend, all you have to do is ask."

"Who says anything's bothering me?"

"People are loners for different reasons. Hurt. Anger. Guilt. I was one myself after my late wife died and I nearly lost the love of my daughter in the process. I hate seeing you go through the same thing."

"Because the town having an EMT is that important."

"No, because you're my friend."

Will met Sam's gaze, then averted his head. No way could he explain his PTSD without looking like a damn wimp. Even to a friend.

"How long will the tour last?" he asked. "I was planning on riding out to the Dividend Mine."

"With this group, I'm thinking an hour should be enough. Two at the most. That'll leave you enough time."

"Getting dark early these days." And the weather was unpredictable at best. "Any chance Luiz can handle the tour?"

At Will's suggestion, Sam had recently added a stop at

the Dividend Mine to their regular trail ride routes. Come spring, a morning of prospecting would be featured as the ranch's newest excursion.

"You're the man for this job," Sam insisted. "These people are special needs. You have the training."

"Right. Because I was once a hospital orderly."

In Sam's eyes, that made Will the resident medical expert. He saw the pieces falling into place. Sam wanted Will to conduct this tour in the hopes of convincing him to accept the town's offer.

"Now that I think about it," Sam continued, "I might have Luiz give you a hand. These folks are a lot to handle."

Now Will's curiosity was really roused. What locals were special needs? Unless…

Sam had been in discussions with the elementary school about hosting field trips for the students. Also with the high school regarding a work-for-class-credit program.

"Look," Will said, "just because I did all right with Trevor and Demi doesn't mean I'm ready to take on a bunch of schoolkids."

"I wouldn't do that to you."

Will's relief was cut short.

"Miranda Staley's arriving with her residents. For an outing. They want to see all the changes."

Great, just great.

"I'd prefer that you let me out of this one," Will said.

"Not possible. I have a wedding to attend."

"You're doing this on purpose."

"What?" Sam feigned innocence.

"It's not going to work, no matter how often you throw Miranda and me together."

"We'll see. This is Sweetheart after all." Sam strode off, grinning.

Chapter Seven

Miranda unbuckled her seat belt and turned off the van's engine in front of the bank. "Be right back."

"I'm going to be late for work," Mrs. Litey complained yet again. For the past hour, since she'd been informed they were visiting the Gold Nugget, she'd mentally returned in time to when she was the ranch's curator. A very conscientious curator, who was rarely late for work.

"This won't take but a minute." In truth, Miranda's tasks were going to require ten, if not fifteen, minutes. In her absence, Nell would keep a watchful eye on the four residents.

"No need to worry yourself." Himey leaned forward from the rear seat and tapped Mrs. Litey's shoulder. "You don't work at the ranch anymore."

Her features instantly collapsed. "I've been fired?"

"Leave her be," Babs snapped, still unhappy that Arthur hadn't been allowed to accompany them on their outing.

Miranda hopped out of the van and slid open the side door. Mrs. Litey sat on the middle bench, closest to the door. She patted the elderly woman's arm reassuringly. "You didn't lose your job. I called ahead and told them we had a stop to make first. Everything's fine."

Mrs. Litey broke into a weepy, grateful smile. "Thank you, Lois."

Miranda had no idea who Lois was and assumed she'd

been a friend or coworker of Mrs. Litey's from years past. "You just sit tight, okay?"

"Where's my purse?"

"On the floor beside you." Miranda reached down, retrieved the heavy purse and placed it on Mrs. Litey's lap. "Here you go."

"Tell Mr. Carter I said hello," Mr. Lexington said from his seat beside Himey. Though none of his companions seemed to care, he elaborated. "I coached his Little League team when he was just a tyke. Worst shortstop you ever saw."

Miranda frowned as she closed the van door. How did Mr. Lexington know she was seeing the loan officer? Big ears, she supposed, and close quarters. Nothing stayed private long in Harmony House.

Clutching the envelope securely in her hand, she made her way inside and to the first available teller station. With more than a little satisfaction, she handed over enough money to cover the two payments due and late fees. Tips at the Paydirt had been good. That, and a small advance from the mayor, had made it possible for Miranda to bring her mortgage current.

For now. In two weeks, she would be scrambling for money again. She tried not to think about it and focus on the positive.

"Here's your receipt." The teller passed Miranda a slip of paper.

"Would you please let Mr. Carter know I'm here?"

"Certainly." The teller buzzed him.

A moment later, he emerged from behind his cubicle wall and beckoned her to join him. Entering the small space, Miranda presented the receipt as if it were a first-place trophy she'd won.

"I'm all caught up with my payments."

"Congratulations." He reviewed the receipt and returned

it to her, his demeanor more reserved than Miranda would have liked.

"Can we refinance my mortgage now?"

"It's not quite that simple. You still have to qualify, and I'm not sure you will."

The exchange of information took more than the ten minutes Miranda had expected, and the paperwork was certainly far from simple. Nell called Miranda's cell phone, questioning how much longer she would be.

"We're almost through." Miranda smiled apologetically at Mr. Carter and disconnected. "The natives are getting restless."

"Have you had any luck finding a fifth resident?"

He would bring that up, naturally. "Not yet, but I'm working on it." She didn't dare tell him about the call from Mr. Lexington's son and the possibility—she prayed a remote one—that his family was going to move him.

She left the building soon after with a stack of documents and a lengthy list of requirements. The next several evenings would be filled with information gathering and at least one trip to the general store for surplus toner. Mr. Carter had requested copies of *everything*.

On the steps outside, she nearly ran over Arthur's daughter and son-in-law, who owned and operated Perfect Fit Tuxedo Rentals. As usual, they were dressed in matching outfits. Today they wore bright red parkas, knit scarves and fur earmuffs. "Mr. and Mrs. Eubanks. How are you?"

"Miranda. It's good to see you." Jody Eubanks enveloped her in a friendly hug. "How was your Thanksgiving?"

"Nice. The usual. Turkey dinner and phone calls to my family. What about you?"

"The kids and grandkids came over. It was simply wonderful."

Miranda recalled Arthur saying his daughters had bickered all day and his grandchildren were spoiled beyond belief. Miranda chose not to contradict Jody. Tolerance for commotion did tend to decrease with age, while tendencies to complain increased.

"Dad's a little put out with you." Jody wagged a finger at Miranda.

"He is?" Her gazed wandered to the van parked a short distance away. She could see Nell through the windshield, attempting to quiet someone. Probably Mrs. Litey. "Why?"

"He wanted terribly to go with you and Babs to the Gold Nugget. Only you said no." Jody's mouth turned down in a pout. "Now he's stuck sitting at home. Alone."

"It's a liability issue. He's not covered under my insurance policy. If anything were to happen…"

Miranda was already taking enough of a risk by allowing Arthur to hang out as much as he did, often past visiting hours. Not to mention the added expense of constantly feeding him. Miranda was too softhearted for her own good.

"You could always drive him to the ranch and meet us there," she said.

"We thought of that, but getting away isn't easy. We've been ridiculously busy lately, what with the contest winners' wedding and outfitting the groom and groomsmen."

Miranda refrained from pointing out that they were away from their shop now. One of them could remain at the shop while the other drove Arthur to the ranch.

"Speaking of which, I should get going."

Jody evidently wasn't done with her. "Dad's miserable when he doesn't see Babs. I wish there was something more we could do."

"Why don't you bring her over to your house for a visit? There's just a simple form you have to sign. I'm sure she'd love it. Arthur, too."

"If we only could. But we have to work."

"I thought you were closed on Wednesdays."

"Everyone needs a day of rest."

Miranda hadn't had a day of rest since last Christmas.

"Caring for one senior citizen is hard enough." Jody appealed to her husband for support. "Two would be, well, twice the work."

Miranda forced a smile. She didn't think she'd met a more self-absorbed woman. "Tell me about it. I have four senior citizens to care for. Five if I count your dad."

"Yes, my dear, but you have help. We don't."

Part-time help. And Miranda was stuck waitressing at the Paydirt Saloon in order to pay for that help.

Resentment built inside her. Considering everything she did for Arthur, Jody didn't act the least bit appreciative, much less offer to compensate Miranda. In fact, if anything, Jody was trying to finagle Miranda into doing more.

Suddenly inspiration struck. "I have a vacancy at the house, if you and Arthur would be interested."

Jody and her husband shared jaw-dropping glances, which they then aimed at Miranda. "Are you suggesting we put Dad in your home? Permanently?"

Miranda kept her voice light. "I could offer adult day care, if you'd rather. Charge you an hourly or daily rate." She was liking the idea more and more.

"We love my father. We wouldn't do that to him," Jody said.

"Do what?" All lightness left Miranda's voice.

"You know. Subject him to that."

Miranda stiffened. "Subject him to what?" A comfortable and safe place to stay? Healthy and delicious meals? Medical supervision? Companionship?

"He wouldn't be happy there." Again Jody turned to her husband.

He just shook his head.

"For someone who's not *happy* there, he spends a considerable amount of time *there*." Miranda pinned Jody with a stare. "You drop him off nearly every day so he can visit Babs."

"That's not the same thing as staying."

Miranda didn't see the difference.

Jody must have finally realized she was offending the sole person responsible for watching her father and making her life infinitely easier, all free of charge.

"I'm sure I've said it before, but thank you." She grabbed her husband's arm, holding it as if to shield herself. "We really do need to get going. Babs will tell Dad all about your trip when he sees her tomorrow."

Miranda had half a mind to tell them no, that Arthur couldn't come over tomorrow, but she didn't. Still, if the refinancing of her mortgage didn't go through, she might have to grow a spine and start standing up to the Eubankses.

WILL WASN'T SURE what was worse, teaching Trevor and Demi to rope or escorting Miranda's residents on a tour of the ranch. Both were an undisciplined lot. And both had a female in charge who was determined to solicit his attention.

There was a difference between the two, however. The cousin/babysitter's attempts had been awkward and painfully obvious. Miranda was considerably more skilled and the effects considerably more effective.

How was it possible for a woman to wear a bulky winter coat and still have curves? She did. At least, the hint of curves was there. Enough to fire Will's imagination.

"Joseph!" Mrs. Litey was the first of Miranda's residents to disembark from the van. Miranda and Nell each supported an arm, assisting the elderly woman to the ground. Her walker followed.

Will had hardly taken a step forward when she advanced, the wheels of her walker scraping over the rough ground.

"Mom." He greeted her with a warm hug. It felt right. Much as holding Miranda felt right.

No, wrong. On both accounts.

His relationship with Mrs. Litey was based on a false-hood, and his one with Miranda was a mistake. He couldn't be the man she wanted. The kind of man she needed. Emotionally whole. Able to love. Able to leave Sweetheart without becoming violently ill.

"What are you doing here at the ranch?" Mrs. Litey asked. "I wasn't expecting you until tonight."

"My flight landed early. Thought I'd surprise you." He'd left Cruze in the barn, afraid Mrs. Litey would be confused by the dog's presence. From what he'd gathered, Joseph hadn't owned a dog.

"You should have called." She brushed his hair from his face, the maternal gesture reminding him of his mother and grandmother.

He bent and kissed her cheek, looking over just in time to catch Miranda watching him as she unloaded Babs's wheelchair. Her expression was unmistakable. He intrigued her.

Will couldn't fathom why. What guy in his right mind kissed a beautiful woman and then left her standing in the cold? Miranda should know better.

"Mom—" he took Mrs. Litey's arm and linked it through his "—mind if I join the tour?"

"Oh, you've seen this old ranch a hundred times."

"Not recently." He propelled her gently along. "Come on."

Convincing her to lead the tour proved an inspiration. She pontificated to the group as if they were tourists rather than her housemates. The newly constructed horse corrals, expanded barn, rodeo arena and four guest cabins threw her, especially when Will took over explaining the additions.

"Why did *The Forty-Niners* cease production?" Miranda asked.

The question instantly grounded Mrs. Litey in her role as guide.

Will shot Miranda a grateful look.

"The studio cited low ratings," Mrs. Litey elaborated. "But most people believe the low ratings resulted from disgruntled fans, most of them women. They didn't like that the story line changed in the last season and that the handsome young son married a, shall we say, soiled dove. They preferred that he and his two equally handsome brothers remain bachelors. The studio was flooded with letters of complaint."

Will was impressed and a little amazed at how vital Mrs. Litey had become. She must have been an excellent guide in her day. It was clear she'd loved her job and the ranch.

"Hard to believe the fans were that fickle," Miranda said. She was in the lead, maneuvering Babs's wheelchair up the walkway to the main house.

"What can you say? A man in a cowboy hat is hard to resist." Mrs. Litey patted the front of Will's jacket. "A man in uniform, too."

"I agree." Miranda glanced over her shoulder at him, her eyes twinkling.

"Now, Lois," Mrs. Litey admonished Miranda, calling her by the wrong name again. "Don't you be entertaining any notions about my Joseph. He's taken."

Will faltered. How did she know about his ex-fiancée? It took him a second to realize that she didn't. Her late son must have had a girlfriend or wife. But why hadn't Mrs. Litey mentioned it before? Will shrugged off his disconcertion.

"All the good ones are," Babs agreed as if she'd been part of the conversation all along. "I'm so lucky to have

Arthur. Can't imagine what I'd do without him. Wish he were here now."

"Maybe next time," Miranda said.

There was an odd note in her voice Will noticed immediately.

The remainder of the tour, lasting another hour, proceeded without a hitch. In the parlor the group went from photograph to photograph hanging on the wall, listening intently to Mrs. Litey recite trivia about the show. At the end she was given an enthusiastic round of applause.

"Thank you and be sure to come back again. Lois, would you see to it that our visitors receive a pamphlet on their way out? Inside is a map of the town and discount coupons for the I Do Café and ice-cream shop."

"Absolutely." Miranda beamed, all trace of whatever was bothering her earlier having vanished.

No one commented on the lack of pamphlets. On the front porch Miranda had trouble navigating Babs's wheelchair down the steps. Nell was too occupied with running herd on the other residents to be of assistance.

"Hold on," she warned as the wheels rocked down the first step.

Babs gasped.

Without thinking, Will stepped in. "Let me."

"I can do it."

He grabbed the handles of the wheelchair, his hands resting behind hers. When she didn't budge, he moved her aside with his body. She still held on.

"Miranda."

She lifted her face to his. "Yes?"

It was then he knew he'd been set up again. This time by her. And he'd fallen for it.

"I've missed you," she whispered and inched closer.

He increased his hold on the wheelchair.

"Don't be a stranger."

To his embarrassment, he gulped.

"Hurry," Babs squeaked.

Will got her down the steps in one piece.

They had barely begun loading up the van when Sam and his family pulled in, his wife behind the wheel. The wedding must be over, though the reception at the Paydirt was expected to last well into the evening.

The red pickup stopped alongside the van, and Sam got out. With a friendly wave, his wife continued down the drive, their three-year-old pressing her face to the window.

"How did it go?" Miranda asked Sam.

"It was nice."

She waited and when he said nothing more, asked, "That's it? Nice?"

"Kinda long. What about you guys?" His glance encompassed the group. "Enjoy yourselves?"

"Men. I swear." Miranda looked injured, as did Babs. "It was a wedding. The most romantic moment in a person's life. And you describe it as nice and long?"

"The food was good."

"The food!"

"We couldn't stay. Annie had to get the girls home."

Miranda slapped her forehead.

Will suppressed a chuckle. He was the one usually in the doghouse for being insensitive and didn't mind sharing it for a change.

"Goodbye, Mom." He hugged Mrs. Litey, and then supported her as she climbed clumsily into the van.

"Joseph?" Gone was the confident and poised curator of the Gold Nugget. In her place was the octogenarian with Alzheimer's.

"It's okay." He patted her affectionately. "Everything will be all right."

"You're a good man." The lines of tension on her face

lessened. "I can't tell you how much I appreciate your visits and humoring an old lady."

For the first time, Will thought she recognized him as himself and wasn't confusing him with her late son. "You're one of my favorite people." He meant every word.

She squeezed his hand. "See you soon?"

"Very soon." Regardless of how he felt about Miranda, he wouldn't disappoint Mrs. Litey.

When all the residents were settled in, he slid the door shut. Nell was next. After giving her a hand up, he tipped his hat and said, "Ma'am."

"Oh, you." She giggled and pushed him away. "Get out of here."

Miranda and Sam were chatting, not about the wedding.

"No, there hasn't been one construction truck parked out front for the past two weeks," she said, apparently in answer to his inquiry. "Thank you for taking care of that."

"Wasn't my intention to cause you problems."

"Boss," Will interrupted, "I'll catch up with you later." He nodded at Miranda. There were three hours of daylight left. More than enough time.

"You heading to the Dividend Mine?" Sam asked.

"I'll clear as much of the trail as I can. Make a list of what more needs doing."

"What's at the Dividend Mine?" Miranda fished her keys from her coat pocket.

"A new excursion for the guests," Sam answered. "Mining for gold."

"Cool! But the Windfall Claim is closer and easier to get to. It's also in an area untouched by the fire. Less debris to clear." She lifted one shoulder. "Just saying."

"I thought the Windfall Claim was privately owned," Sam said.

"It was. Until a few years ago. The claim, that entire section of land, actually, was sold to the federal government when the owner died. His heirs didn't want it."

"And, because it's federal land—"

"It's open to the public," Miranda finished for Sam.

"Are you by chance looking for a job? I can use a good mining guide."

"Very funny."

He grinned. "I like the way you think, Miranda. What about you, Will?"

"It's a good idea." It *was* a good idea. "Except for that one slope along the western face. It's steep. Maybe too steep for our less experienced riders."

"You can bypass the slope. There's a shortcut."

"Where?"

"The Ten Mile Trail."

"Never heard of it." Will had ridden the mountains surrounding Sweetheart nearly every day for the past five years. If there was a trail to be ridden, he'd done it.

"It's not well-known. Intersects with the Spur Cross Trail along the north half, at the base of Grey Rock Point. My father used to take us kids there when the land was privately owned. He wasn't supposed to, but he did anyway."

"I can't picture it."

"Me, either," Sam agreed.

"I could show you," Miranda offered. "The Windfall Claim really is a lot closer to the ranch. And the stream there is plenty deep enough for your guests to pan for gold."

"You willing to take Miranda with you?" Sam asked Will.

Not what he wanted, but he could hardly say no in front of his boss. "When's your next day off?"

"I could go now. Nell will drive the van back."

"Now?"

Sam jumped on the bandwagon. "Great! You can ride, right?"

"Been a while." Miranda laughed. "But as long as you don't give me a bronc, I'll manage."

"What are you waiting for?" Sam slapped Will on the back. "Saddle up."

Yeah, saddle up, Will thought, feeling completely ambushed.

Miranda and Sam together were an unstoppable force.

Chapter Eight

Miranda knew enough not to fire questions at Will. He wouldn't answer them anyway. She and Sam had coerced Will into taking her along with him. Not the best way to go about loosening his tongue.

She settled for riding quietly behind him down the winding drive from the ranch to the main road. There they hugged the side, avoiding the occasional passing vehicle.

Patches of snow from the last flurry still covered the ground. If the next storm was as bad as the weathercasters were predicting, the mountains would soon be impassable.

He turned in his saddle, one hand braced on the back, the other holding the reins. His body rocked in rhythm to the horse's easy gait. "You doing okay?"

Conversation. Well, well.

"Just dandy." She smiled winningly. Once he resumed looking straight ahead, she grimaced.

What had she done? Wanting to spend time alone with Will had skewed her thinking. Her knees were already starting to throb and her calves ached.

Miranda hadn't lied to Sam—she'd spent a great part of her youth riding friends' horses. Her youth, not her recent past. She was definitely out of shape—at least the muscles required for riding were out of shape.

And she was cold! Her lightweight gloves had been fine

for touring the ranch. But they were practically worthless when it came to a winter horse ride in the mountains.

They turned onto the well-marked Spur Cross trailhead. "How far is the junction with Ten Mile Trail?" Will asked.

"About another quarter mile." And then it would be mostly uphill from there. Fabulous. She'd be adding a sore back to her list of complaints by the time they reached the Windfall Claim site.

She needed something to take her mind off the ride. Disregarding her previous conviction not to pester Will, she said, "Tell me about her."

"Who?"

"The girl. Woman. Your ex. Whatever she was."

"I don't know what you're talking about."

Liar. His jacket did nothing to hide the sudden tension squaring his shoulders.

"When Mrs. Litey said you were taken, you went three shades paler."

"She was referring to Joseph."

"Probably, though I'm not convinced she's as forgetful as she appears. But that has nothing to do with your reaction. I'm curious. Who's the woman who broke Will Dessaro's heart?"

"Who's Lois?"

Nice try, Miranda thought. "I'll tell if you tell."

"No deal."

Undaunted, she continued. "Lois is someone Mrs. Litey worked with years ago. So, ex-girlfriend? Ex-wife? Ex-*lover*?"

He remained diligently silent.

"Tell you what. I'll guess, and you let me know if I'm right." She took her first stab in the dark. "This all happened before you came to Sweetheart."

Still nothing.

No matter, Miranda was fairly confident. She'd made

enough inquiries about Will the past few months, and not a single person had mentioned a local girlfriend, even a casual one. Which made no sense. Guys as ruggedly handsome as him were usually fighting off female admirers.

She studied him as they rode, when she wasn't watching the ever steepening slope. "Someone from high school? College?" She paused a beat. "The army?"

More tension.

Will didn't need to talk much. His body language and facial expressions revealed his every thought and emotion. Also, the tone of his voice.

"Okay, the army. Was she a civilian or in the military?"

"Neither."

"Military, then," she decided.

Will ducked to avoid a low tree limb stretching across the trail.

"Definitely military." Miranda ducked to avoid the same tree limb. "Did you serve together? How long did you date? Why did you break up?"

"I'm not talking about this," he snapped.

"She must have really hurt you. Enough that you haven't dated anyone in years and refuse to talk about her. Did your PTSD have anything to do with it?"

As far as conversation killers went, she'd picked a zinger. Will clammed up. Miranda fumed. All right, she shouldn't have pried. He was entitled to his privacy.

Long seconds of silence stretched into minutes until they reached the junction. There she advised Will to take the right fork.

"That trail dead-ends," he argued.

"It zigzags." Miranda strove to lighten the mood and teased, "Want me to go first?"

His scowl could only be described as affronted.

The horses climbed the steep slope, lowering their

heads for balance and placing their feet carefully among the craggy rocks.

"This incline won't be nearly so difficult in better weather," Miranda commented. "Your guests will do fine, even the less experienced riders."

At the top, they stopped to rest the horses. Miranda looked around for the Ten Mile trailhead. Thanks to overgrown brush and half a lifetime since she'd last visited these parts, it wasn't easy to find. She was about to suggest they continue the search on foot when she spotted the narrow opening.

A small yelp of glee escaped her. "There! See?" She nudged her horse through the opening, taking the lead.

Will didn't admit it, but she thought he might be a little impressed. Score one for her.

The shortcut paid off. Fifteen minutes later they reached the Windfall Claim site. A broken wooden sluice box sat not far from the icy stream, hardly more than a pile of timbers. Beside it was a rusty shovel, the head of an ax and a rotted canvas tarp that probably sheltered hordes of insects. Remnants from more modern prospectors.

Will dismounted with ease. Miranda, not so much. Her sore joints and cold stiff hands hampered her. On the ground her legs gave out, and she grabbed the side of the saddle seconds before tumbling. All at once Will was beside her.

"Steady there." He supported her arm.

Sweet Lord in heaven, she loved the sound of his voice when he wasn't annoyed at her. She let its timbre slide over her.

"I'm such a klutz."

"You're anything but a klutz." His hand moved slowly from her elbow up her arm, where it lingered. His eyes, so brown they appeared black, remained fastened on her for endless moments.

If he asked, she would tell him anything. Reveal her deepest secrets.

"We, um, should probably tie up the, uh, horses."

Her, shy? Seriously? Miranda was the queen of confidence.

"After that climb, they're too tired to go anywhere." His strong fingers squeezed her flesh through her coat sleeve. "Trust me."

"I do." She trembled slightly.

"You cold?" His arm circled her, drew her close. "I've got a poncho in my saddlebag."

"Uh-uh." She shook her head. What was with the short answers? That was Will's style, not hers.

"Well, if you change your mind…" He dipped his head.

He was going to kiss her. She closed her eyes in anticipation, whispered his name on a half breath.

Nothing happened. What the…?

She opened her eyes to find him staring intently at her and stiffened. "My mistake." How embarrassing!

He anchored her more solidly to him and, with his hand, pressed the side of her face to his chest. The jacket's rough fabric scratched her cheek, but she didn't pull back.

"Yes," he said.

She sensed rather than saw him staring off into the distance. "Yes, what?"

"You're right," he admitted at last. "About everything. I met her in the army, and she dumped me cold when she found out about my PTSD."

"Oh, Will. I'm sorry." Instead of feeling jubilation over getting him to open up, Miranda's throat tightened. She herself had endured heartaches over relationships gone wrong more than once. "That must have been awful."

He tilted her face to his, and she readied herself. This time he would kiss her for sure.

Wrong again. Instead of taking her into his arms, he

moved her gently aside and patted her head as if she were a child.

"We'd better check out the claim site while there's still plenty of daylight left."

WILL HAD A problem. He couldn't get within two feet of Miranda without wanting to take her in his arms and kiss her. As if that was news.

Up until recently he'd been able to resist. But it was getting harder. If not for him suddenly coming to his senses, he might have acted on his impulses.

Another disaster narrowly avoided. Their third one today. Will was getting good at it. What he should be doing, however, was steering clear of potentially dangerous situations altogether. Ones that put him and Miranda in close proximity.

Such as visiting Mrs. Litey. Accompanying Miranda to the ice-cream shop. Bringing her on horse rides where she could get chilled or stumble and need to be held.

"I'm sorry for being nosy."

She'd come up behind him while he was wrapping Rocket Dog's reins around the saddle horn. Miranda's horse was already loose and picking through the shallow layer of snow with its hooves, searching for anything edible that had survived.

"It's all right."

"Sometimes I let my big mouth get the better of me."

"I hadn't noticed." He delivered the barb good-naturedly.

"If you'd like, I can tell you about when my birth parents abandoned me. Even the score."

"Maybe someday." Will wanted to hear about her childhood. Her college days. Her stint at the hospital in Reno, and how she came to open Harmony House.

But then she'd want to get to know him better, too, and he'd already revealed too much. Time to draw the line. Will was not good boyfriend material. He'd learned that lesson already with Lexie.

Giving Rocket Dog's rump a pat, he let her join her buddy and started toward the wrecked sluice, Miranda keeping pace with him. "Is any of this usable?" he asked.

"You're better off building a new one. They aren't hard. My dad could give you a set of plans."

With the babble of running water in the background, they sorted through the array of discarded prospecting equipment. Will would have to pack it down the mountain on horseback. Getting a vehicle up here would be impossible. Even an ATV. Then he'd have to haul the new equipment in. Quite a project.

"The Chinese developed a different kind of sluice called a rocker." Miranda removed a broken timber from the pile and turned it over, exposing the sharp rusted nail points on the underside. "Some operations were fairly sophisticated. Most prospectors started out with a simple pan and went from there. If they were smart, they invested a portion of their finds in better equipment."

"You ever pan for gold up here?"

"With my dad. I was pretty good at it, too. Better than my brothers and sisters."

"You had the knack."

"I had the patience. It's tedious work."

"I thought you said the federal government didn't acquire the land until recently."

"That's true." She smiled coyly.

"You prospected illegally?"

"If you ask my dad, he'll tell you we were conducting studies."

Will thought he might like Miranda's dad.

"We never found more than some particles. Enough to whet our appetites." She knelt by the creek, removed her glove and dipped her fingers in the icy water. "What about you? Ever try?"

"A few times when I first arrived in Sweetheart. I gave up quickly."

"It's pretty labor-intensive."

"Clearing this place is going to be labor-intensive, too. There a lot of junk to haul off."

Miranda stood and dried her hand on her jeans. "I think you should leave everything as it is. Gives the place authenticity. In fact, you should bring even more old equipment up here. The guests will love it. Lots of photo ops."

She had a point.

"You could make arrangements with the general store. They carry all kinds of prospecting equipment. Your guests could rent the equipment from the store. The ranch would get a cut, of course."

Smart *and* pretty. Will was in bigger trouble than he thought.

"You sure you don't need a third job?"

"I might if I can't refinance my mortgage."

"How's that going?"

"Ask me next week."

"What about your dad? You said he's retired."

"Nah, he and Mom won't leave Reno." Her blue eyes, the color of winter, sparkled. "My brother Nash might be interested. He's only available in the summers, though."

"He's a teacher?"

"A ski instructor and wilderness guide at Diamond Peak Resort. I could give you his number."

They continued exploring the old mining operation. Will found he enjoyed seeing it through Miranda's eyes. Her knowledge was impressive. What took him aback the most was how easily conversation flowed between them. He couldn't remember the last time he'd talked this much.

Not even with Mrs. Litey, whom he felt more comfortable with than anyone else.

Now and then his and Miranda's arms brushed. She ignored it while Will braced himself for a panic attack. None came. Could he be getting better? More likely he was developing a tolerance to her.

He watched her unearth a bolt with the toe of her boot and stoop to pick it up. His pulse spiked. Not from panic. Rather it was from the memory of holding her and kissing her.

Desire and alarm. Funny, he hadn't noticed how similar the two physical responses were.

"Watch you don't slip," he warned when she returned to the creek to wash off the bolt. "The bank's muddy."

"Will you catch me if I do?"

He'd catch her, all right, and once he had her, he'd...

She tossed the bolt onto the sluice. "I can meet with you if you want."

"Meet?"

"Talk about your guests panning for gold. How to set up the operation."

"Sure." The stab of disappointment he felt was acute. And wrong.

"Or we could just go out. On a date. You and me."

Her hopeful smile almost swayed him. "Miranda—"

"Don't say no."

"I have to."

"I told you. I don't care about your PTSD."

If he was going to take a chance with anyone, it would be her. But the risk was too great. Of hurting her and disappointing her and, worse, the very real likelihood she'd leave him when she discovered his limitations.

"I'm not like your ex-fiancée," she said. "I'm a nurse. I could help."

Her having familiarity with his disorder didn't make

him feel better. There would be no minimizing or glossing over the truth with her.

"You've seen therapists before." She swept the debris from an overturned log and perched on it. There was room for two. "Someone taught you coping techniques."

Will didn't join her—he needed to stand. Their conversation was no longer easy. "A few times over the years."

"What treatments have you tried?"

"Hypnosis. Meditation. Redecision therapy. EMDR."

"Eye movement desensitization and reprocessing. That's pretty intense. Did it help?"

"To a degree."

"Then you stopped all treatment when you came to Sweetheart."

"Stopped and regressed." He'd convinced himself he only needed a little space and solitude to heal.

But weeks turned into months and months into years. Shutting himself off had become a habit. An addiction. The fire, evacuating Miranda's residents, had changed everything.

"Your PTSD started when your parents died?"

The last time Will had talked about this was with his ex-fiancée. So long ago. So much had transpired.

"Will?"

His jaw had frozen shut.

"There's only us here," she said softly. "I promise, I won't tell a soul."

Her words weren't unlike those of his therapists. Did everyone in the medical profession get the same training? Putting Patients At Ease 101?

"How old were you?" she prompted.

"Sixteen."

"Were your parents in an accident?"

"Automobile. We were on vacation." Once started, he couldn't stop. The story poured from him with a will of its own. "Driving through Yellowstone National Park. There'd been a thunderstorm that day. The roads were wet. A herd of elk suddenly ran out from the trees and in front of the car. Dad swerved to avoid them."

Will covered his ears. They rang with the violent sounds of the crash. Searing pain shot through him from the impact of being slammed into the car roof. His body went rigid as he soared through the air and hit the ground with a bone-crunching thud. There was a moment of blackness, and then he could see again. Could speak again.

"Are you okay?" Miranda asked.

He cleared his throat, wiped at the sweat on his forehead. "I was ejected from the car about halfway down the ravine. Either the door sprang or I opened it. I don't remember. When the car hit bottom about a hundred feet down, it exploded. I tried, but I couldn't get to my parents in time." He squeezed his eyes closed. "They were too far away, and my right ankle was shattered. I watched the car go up in flames, praying they died instantly and didn't suffer."

"The accident wasn't your fault, Will."

"I know that."

"Survivor guilt isn't easy to conquer."

"Did I survive?" He looked at Miranda then, his heart in pieces. "Or did I save myself and let them die?"

"You're lucky to have gotten out alive."

"I don't feel lucky. I should have done more. Stayed with them. Tried to climb down to the car."

"And died, too? That's not what they would have wanted."

More familiar words. Will hated hearing them. "The panic attacks started after the funeral."

"Is that why you don't want to be an EMT?"

"I can't let more people down."

"You didn't let your parents down. They'd tell you that if they could."

"But they can't. They're not here."

Miranda gave him a moment to collect himself. "Where did you live after they died?"

"With my grandmother."

"Tell me about her."

"She had a farm. Raised soybeans and alfalfa. That's where I learned to ride. She saved me. Her and the horses."

"Did you rodeo?"

"Some. Locally. My grandmother had other ideas for me. She was determined I get an education. I went to community college, got my associates degree in equine sciences."

"How did you wind up in the army?"

"My grandmother died."

Miranda made a sound of distress. "Not an accident, I hope."

"Natural causes. A heart attack. No one saw it coming. She was in perfect health."

"Heart conditions can go undetected for years."

"That's what the doctors told me."

"You don't blame yourself for her death, do you?"

"I wasn't there when she had the heart attack."

There was a pause, and then Miranda guessed, "You found her." She was too astute for her own good.

"On the kitchen floor. She'd been gone for hours." He shuddered, reliving that awful moment. "I should have been there."

"You said yourself, no one saw it coming."

"She was a good person. A kind person. She deserved more than to die alone."

"She didn't. You loved her and were there with her in spirit."

Will wasn't consoled. He missed his grandmother and his parents. He wanted this conversation to stop so he could go back to the emotional cave where the pain was bearable.

Miranda wouldn't let him. "You joined the army to get away."

He nodded.

"How did you manage with your disorder?"

"They kept me busy. On track. Because of my studies, they assigned me to hospital duty. I liked it."

"Didn't working in a hospital trigger your PTSD?"

"At first. I got better at coping."

"Then you met your ex-fiancée."

"Those were the best two years of my life since my parents died. Our enlistments were due to be up about the same time. We were going to get married, move back to Kansas and run my grandmother's farm."

"Except you had a panic attack." Miranda proved her astuteness once again.

"My first in twenty months."

"What triggered it?"

"A captain and his wife were brought into the E.R. DOA. Their vehicle had gone off the road. There was no explosion—they died from internal injuries. It was still enough like my parents' accident to set me off. I kept it together till I got off duty, then I went straight to my barracks. She was there waiting for me. Had no idea what was happening. Freaked her out. The next day she sent me an email. Said she couldn't handle my disorder. She re-upped. I didn't."

"Did you see her again?"

"No reason to. A few weeks later, my discharge came through. I packed up my duffel bag, sold my grandmother's farm and came to Sweetheart. Along the way I found Cruze and adopted him. He's seen me through some bad times."

"Why Sweetheart and not Kansas?"

"I wanted to start over in a place where no one knew me or my history. Someplace remote. Where a person who's a loner doesn't stand out." He didn't tell her about his inability to leave Sweetheart. She'd think him certifiable.

"Shutting yourself off from people isn't the answer, Will." She stood and came to him.

"It's worked so far."

"But are you happy?" She sought his gaze.

"I'm functioning. That's what's important."

"You're punishing yourself."

"Don't analyze me, Miranda," he snapped. "I've had enough of that." She was digging too deep, getting perilously close to uncovering all his secrets.

"You're right. I'm sorry." She put some space between them. "I'd still want to help if you'll let me."

"No offense, but your specialty is old people."

"The elderly have a lot of issues, including stress. Often acute stress."

"It's not the same."

"It's also not that different. I could do some research. Contact the doctors in the Reno hospital where I worked. Ask their advice."

She was being sweet and thoughtful. She was also interfering.

"Thanks, but no."

"Are you afraid?"

"Hell, yes, I'm afraid. You have no idea what it's like. Losing control. Convinced you're going to die."

"I do have an idea. I felt that way when my birth parents left me in a car for three straight days when I was just seven."

"It's not the same."

"Let me help, Will."

"Do you really not understand?"

"Apparently not."

"You're one of the triggers that causes me to lose control."

She digested that information for a moment. "The kiss. That's why you left so suddenly."

He was finished spilling his guts. "It's getting dark. We need to leave." Will didn't mind riding at night. Miranda might not be as keen.

Gathering the horses, he led them over to the clearing where it was easier to mount. Miranda was shivering again.

Without asking, he unbuckled one of his saddlebags and removed the rain poncho. While thin, the plastic would afford some protection. "Here."

"I'm okay."

"It's only going to get colder during the ride."

"Fine."

He shook out the poncho and placed it over her head, then fastened the snap at the neck. Their gazes locked. Held.

"Thank you." Her voice was low. Inviting. Was it intentional?

"You're welcome."

There was no reason on the face of the earth for him to continue standing there. Every reason to put distance between them. Hadn't he just given her several?

"You don't know how badly I wish things were different," he said.

"Maybe they could be. If you tried."

Lord, she was tempting. Cheeks and nose tinged pink by the cold. Lips full and lush.

Will was strong. He could resist. He'd done it earlier.

Only he hadn't counted on what she said next.

"Are you going to kiss me?" She lifted her face to his. "Or make me stand here all night?"

Chapter Nine

"Take a chance, Will." She clutched the front of his jacket and stood on tiptoes. Her breath was warm, her gaze hot.

Adrenaline spread through him like wildfire, setting every nerve on fire. His hands shook. His heart pounded.

Desire. Not panic. He was learning to tell the difference.

Temptation beckoned. He might have held out, but then her lips parted and he was a goner. Gripping her shoulders, he hauled her to him.

He was going to pay for this, one way or another. With luck she'd be done with him. Just like Lexie. Maybe it was for the best.

"You think too much," Miranda said, and she was right.

Will claimed her, quickly taking charge of the kiss. Angling his head, he bent her back and plunged his tongue deep in her mouth. If he didn't scare her off with a panic attack, he would with his ardor.

God help him, she wasn't intimidated. Molding her body to his, she took what he gave and made demands in return. Will increased the pressure. She responded by slipping her hands beneath his jacket and circling his waist.

He was doomed. Stopping was impossible.

Cupping her cool cheek in his palm, he slid his fingers under her knit cap and into her hair. It was like silk, fine and smooth as spun gold. He'd dreamed about touching it.

Burying his face in it. Watching the blond strands glide across his bare chest.

Did she know the profound effect she had on him? To erase all doubt, he showed her, and wasn't satisfied until he'd wrenched a needy moan from her that nearly sent him over the edge.

She broke off the kiss only to speak his name against his lips. Will crushed her to him, his heart on the verge of exploding.

No, not on the verge. Already there.

He backed away as his lungs compressed, squeezing out the last molecule of oxygen. His field of vision narrowed to a pinpoint. Terror consumed him. Weakened him.

"Will, are you all right?"

He heard Miranda but didn't answer her. Couldn't push the words past the invisible fists strangling him. Bending forward, he hugged his middle and let the attack run its course.

Served him right for letting Miranda in.

"Will!" She shook his arm. Really shook it and barked sharply, "That's enough."

Enough? He'd stop this nightmare if he could.

She grabbed his chin with enough strength that pain shot through his jaw, forcing him to meet her gaze. "Stop this, you hear me?"

Not exactly the kind and compassionate treatment he'd expect from a nurse. And yet, the panic receded slightly. She didn't let go of him, didn't look away. She made him focus on her and kept repeating, "Stop this now."

Eventually the air surrounding them thinned and became breathable. The fists choking him released their hold.

"Better?" she asked.

He was, his speedy recovery a complete surprise. "Yeah, I'm okay."

Her posture immediately deflated.

Perhaps his plan to discourage her had succeeded after all. She looked scared to death. Who could blame her?

"Sorry about that," he said.

"Don't be. Parts of it were quite good."

"Are you that tough with Mrs. Litey when she has an episode?"

"I'm never afraid she's going to stroke out on me."

Will didn't return her teasing. He wasn't in the mood. He'd just exposed his demons to someone for the first time in five years and had no idea how he stood with that person.

Fortunately the falling darkness hid his features, or Miranda would have read him like a book.

Falling darkness! Wait. How late was it?

"We need to leave," he said. "While we can still find our way down the mountain."

She didn't argue. They mounted up and Will took the lead. The trail was steep in places, made more difficult by the lack of daylight. He looked back often to check on her progress but said nothing.

The horses proved their worth and carried them safely to the main road. A half mile from the ranch, Sam called Will, concerned that they weren't home yet. Will assured his boss all was well, though it didn't feel that way. Miranda hadn't spoken more than two sentences on the entire return ride.

At the corrals, their conversation remained limited to the necessities. Did she require any help dismounting? Where should she tie up her horse? What about unsaddling? Will assured her he'd take care of everything.

He hadn't thought about how she'd get home until a car pulled up with one of the servers from the Paydirt behind the wheel.

"I called Cissy when you were in the tack shed," she said, responding to his silent question. "Asked her for a lift."

"I'd have driven you home."

"You have a lot to do. I didn't want to impose."

Or she wanted to get away from him as quickly as possible.

She turned to leave, stopping after a few steps. "I shouldn't have pushed you so hard. I apologize."

He shrugged. "Just as you said, parts of it were good."

"What parts, Will? Just the kiss?"

He thought carefully about it before answering. "No. Talking was good, too." Grueling. Agonizing. Embarrassing. Depleting. But good.

"I'm glad."

She left, the taillights of her friend's car growing smaller before disappearing altogether.

Will finished brushing the horses and put them up for the night, making sure they were well fed. Fetching Cruze from the barn, he walked the corrals and the livestock pens, as was his routine before going home.

Miranda had helped him. He'd resisted, and she'd persisted. This panic attack had been less intense than his previous ones.

If he didn't see her again, if he'd scared her off as he had suspected, he'd always be grateful for that.

"HONEST TO GOODNESS," Cissy gushed, "when have you ever seen so many good-looking men gathered in one place?"

They were at the Paydirt, in the middle of their shifts.

"Not for a while," Miranda had to admit. "Once at the hospital, a bus carrying a minor league baseball team was in an accident. A couple of the players were hurt. Not seriously. The whole team showed up in the waiting room."

"Lucky you." Cissy loaded her tray with mugs of beer and tumblers of whiskey as fast as the bartender could pour them.

"There were some cuties."

In Miranda's opinion, none of them had been better looking than the group assembled. Cliff Dempsey and Sam

Wyler were heading the first official meeting of the newly recruited Sweetheart Volunteer Fire Department. Will was in attendance, along with four other young to middle-aged men. The mayor and two representatives of the town council had joined them. The council secretary sat at a neighboring table, taking notes on a laptop.

"Your fellow over there's watching you." Cissy sauntered off with the tray.

"He's not my fellow," Miranda called after her, then promptly shut her mouth. Had anyone besides Cissy heard her?

She glanced in Will's direction. He *was* watching her. Although it was hard to read his expression at this distance, she was pretty sure he wasn't pining after her.

To Miranda's dismay, news of her and Will's kiss outside the Paydirt a few weeks ago had spread. Someone had seen them and had blabbed on their next visit to the saloon. That was all it took. Cissy wasn't the only one giving Miranda a hard time.

Thank goodness no one had seen them kissing a second time at the Windfall Claim site.

Miranda didn't care. Will, however, did. He tried not to let the ribbing he'd been receiving from the other patrons bother him. Anyone who knew him at all could see that it did. And then she'd gone and made things worse by pressuring him to open up. Not to mention throwing herself at him on top of that. No wonder the poor guy had suffered a panic attack.

She'd yet to decide how she felt about their awkward parting and future relationship—not that there was much potential for one. Dwelling on it for three days hadn't given her an answer. It was a classic battle between head and heart.

Her head said it was a lost cause. She should do as he wanted and forget about them.

Her heart said she shouldn't give up. Their chemistry was off the charts and worth fighting for.

The volunteer firefighters' meeting got underway, with the mayor and sheriff taking turns leading the discussion. It was a slow afternoon at the Paydirt, too late for the lunch crowd and too early for the after-work crowd.

Miranda had been assigned the job of decorating the Christmas tree. Truth be told, she'd offered to do it. The tree was tucked in an area next to the stage and to the right of the restrooms. Personally, she considered the location a disaster waiting to happen, but the mayor had insisted. Someone, probably several someones, was going to knock over the tree in their haste to reach the lavatory.

Location aside, Miranda took pleasure in the task. She'd decorated Harmony House inside and out, top to bottom. Lights, wreaths, garland, lawn ornaments. It had given her an outlet on which to expend the nervous energy building up from thinking too much about Will.

He'd visited once in the past three days to see Mrs. Litey. Miranda had been at the Paydirt, something she suspected was planned on his part. It was easy enough to find out her schedule.

"Don't forget the mistletoe," the bartender reminded her when she made yet another trip to the storeroom. "The mayor wants it hung from the chandelier."

"Right."

The chandelier, crafted from an antique wagon wheel, was suspended from the rafter just inside the front entrance. Miranda carted the stepladder with her from the storeroom, snatching the sprig of green and red mistletoe off the corner of the bar as she passed.

Of course, it reminded her of kissing Will and how wrong that had gone. Both times.

Argh! She had to stop thinking of him or she was going to wear out her brain.

Whatever had given her the notion to practice armchair psychology without understanding the full extent of his condition first? And she called herself a nurse.

Even with the stepladder, she had to stretch her arms to their longest length to reach the chandelier. Her fingers fumbled, and she dropped the mistletoe.

"Need a hand?"

She started at the deep masculine voice and steadied herself before looking down.

Sam grinned up at her, the sprig in his hand.

Not Will. What a relief. Not that she'd expected him to come over. "What about the meeting?"

"We're taking a break for a few minutes while the secretary researches some equipment prices online."

Miranda sneaked a peak at Will. He sat at the table, staring into his beer. No longer at her. That was good, right? "Sure. Thanks. I'm either too short or the chandelier's too high."

Sam took her place on the stepladder and easily attached the mistletoe. "How's this?"

"Great. Appreciate the assistance."

Sam climbed down the ladder and, with no warning whatsoever, kissed her soundly on the cheek.

Her fingers automatically flew to the spot as a small gasp escaped. "What was that for?"

"We are standing under mistletoe."

"Seriously, Sam." She didn't believe him for one second.

His answer was to incline his head at the table where the meeting was taking place.

She spun. Will was staring at them. She felt the intensity of his gaze despite the distance separating them.

"I still don't understand," she stammered.

"I'm proving a point." Sam winked at her. "He cares about you."

"He may."

"He *does*."

"Regardless, he and I—"

"Miranda, you're good for him."

She shook her head, recalling the night on the mountain. "You don't know how wrong you are."

"I'm willing to bet differently." He left her then, his long strides taking him across the room to rejoin the meeting.

Miranda didn't move. She was too stunned to do anything else. The sound of her cell phone ringing roused her from her stupor. Removing it from her pocket, she checked the number and bit her lip. Mr. Lexington's son. Normally she didn't take calls while on duty at the Paydirt, except for emergencies. This could be one.

"Hello, Gary."

"Miranda, how are you?"

At his tone, her stomach plummeted. She walked to the corner, seeking privacy. "You tell me. Have you and your brothers made a decision?"

"We did."

She could hear the answer in his voice, and all hope evaporated.

"I'm sorry. We have to do what's best for Dad."

A second's worth of preparation didn't make a difference. She took the news badly.

"I understand." But she didn't. Not at all. Mr. Lexington wouldn't be happy living away from Sweetheart. Gary was doing what was best for him. "Have you told him?"

"Not yet. We're thinking of coming up this weekend unannounced and moving him. That way he'll have less time to fret and become anxious."

"Gary." Miranda was aghast. "I can't tell you what a mistake I think that is. He needs to be told. Have the chance to say his goodbyes and finalize any business."

"This coming weekend is the only one I have free for the next two months." He sounded a bit put off.

She tried a different approach. "In my experience with elderly residents, they don't always adjust well to change. Abrupt change is even harder."

"My point exactly. You know how he is. He'll procrastinate. Come up with every excuse in the book as to why we shouldn't move him. Dig in his heels."

"He'll do that anyway. This is his home."

"Dad loves visiting us. He'll make the transition."

He'd do better with advance notice. "I'm asking you to reconsider." Miranda pressed her free hand to her forehead. "At least wait till after the holidays." She could figure out something by then. Hopefully have refinanced her mortgage.

"I'm sorry," Gary repeated, without a trace of sympathy.

"So am I."

"Don't say a word to Dad. Promise me."

"I wouldn't go behind your back." She may completely disagree with him, but she would abide by his wishes.

"I didn't mean to imply anything. You've been good to Dad. This is hard on all of us."

She chided herself for being selfish. Caring for an elderly parent wasn't easy, and there were often difficult decisions that had to be made. Unfortunately, she would bear the brunt of this particular decision.

"What time will you be arriving on Saturday?" she asked.

Trying not to let her dismal financial situation color the rest of her conversation with Gary, they finalized the arrangements. Miranda hung up, thinking she would have to give Nell notice. With only three residents, she was either going to have to put in more hours at the Paydirt or cut back on Nell's hours.

Neither choice was desirable, but reducing Nell's hours made the most sense. It was silly for Miranda to work an outside job just to pay Nell's wages.

Brushing at her damp cheeks—when had she started to cry?—she pocketed her phone and returned to the Christmas tree. The twinkling lights did nothing to lift her spirits this time.

"Hey."

Another masculine voice sounded from behind her, this one also giving her a start. *Not now, please,* she thought.

"Hi, Will." She fiddled with a candy-cane ornament that was drooping to one side. "Aren't you supposed to be in the meeting?"

"We're on break."

"Didn't you just have one?" How did they get any work done?

"Actually, I ditched the meeting." His expression wasn't the least bit contrite.

"Won't you get in trouble?"

"I don't care." He shifted, which somehow brought him closer to her. "Did your phone call not go well?"

She should be flattered that he was paying so much attention to her. Fifteen minutes ago she would have been. But then Gary had called and she'd gone from barely making ends meet to the very real possibility of losing her home.

The savings and loan simply *had* to approve her refinancing. When Miranda turned in the paperwork on Tuesday, Mr. Carter had told her the process would take a few days.

"Mr. Lexington's son called," she told Will. "He's moving his dad in with him."

"When?"

"This weekend."

"Wow." Will pushed his hat back on his head. "That's not much notice."

"Yeah." Tears returned to her eyes. She blinked them away.

"What are you going to do?"

"I'm not sure." Miranda fiddled with the candy-cane ornament. Now instead of drooping to the left, it drooped to the right. She sighed. Would nothing go right? "I was hoping Arthur's family would agree to an adult day-care arrangement. One that involved compensating me."

"They should. He's there a lot."

"I doubt they will." Miranda made a face. "I kind of ticked them off the other day."

Will placed a hand on her shoulder, the gesture comforting. Friend to friend.

Who needed words? He did just fine without them. Miranda leaned toward him.

"I… We…"

"No kiss. Just a hug. Okay? I can't take anything else." He folded her in his embrace.

She rested her face on his chest. The moment didn't last. Her cell phone rang again. She would have let the call go to voice mail, but Will gently eased her away from him.

"Better get that," he said.

She checked the display and her disinterest changed to excitement, then trepidation. "It's the savings and loan."

"Answer it." He left her to take the call in private.

She pressed the phone to her ear and retreated to the same corner as earlier. "Hello?"

"Ms. Staley? This is Ruth from Northern Nevada Savings and Loan. Mr. Carter asked me to call you."

"Yes?" Miranda swallowed, dismayed at how high and thin her voice sounded. "Has my refinancing been approved?"

"Mr. Carter wants to meet with you, if you're available."

"When?"

"He has an opening tomorrow morning at eleven-thirty."

"I'll be there." She was scheduled to work the afternoon shift at the Paydirt. Nell was arriving at noon. Miranda would have to coerce her into coming early.

"Very good. I'll let Mr. Carter know."

Miranda swore there was a smile in the woman's voice. Her refinance request must have been approved. Mr. Carter wouldn't want to see her just to tell her no. He'd send a letter.

She returned to decorating the tree, feeling a hundred pounds lighter. When Will looked at her from the table where he sat, she smiled, telegraphing her hope. He answered with a thumbs-up.

She'd still need to find a new resident to replace Mr. Lexington. Two would be better. But with a lower mortgage payment, she had a little more time.

As if giving her a sign, the candy-cane ornament hung perfectly straight.

Chapter Ten

"What do you think? Isn't she a beauty?" Sam passed his smartphone across the desk to the mayor for her inspection. "The Bishop County Fire Department emailed this photo to me yesterday."

The mayor took the phone and studied the picture of the fire engine, her face reflecting her delight. "Very nice."

Will had seen the photo already. His reaction was slightly less enthralled. All right, considerably less. He understood Sam and the mayor's excitement. An improved volunteer fire department would provide a real boon to the town.

If only he felt more confident about being an asset to the department and not a detriment.

He and Sam had come to town in order to pick up a pallet of grain at the feed store. Once that task had been accomplished, Sam had dropped by the mayor's office, revealing the real reason for their spontaneous errand run.

"Is it for sale?" the mayor asked hopefully.

"Not any longer. They found a buyer." Sam looked ready to burst. "Me."

"Hot dog!" The mayor threw her arms up in the air. "Tell me everything. All the details."

"It's a pumper-tanker engine. Only six years old." Sam spoke with the kind of reverence one might use when describing a rare work of art. "It has an impeller water-pump system and a built-in thousand-gallon tank."

"Where did you find it?"

Sam explained his efforts over the past few days to the mayor. The results had been a fire engine that was within the town's budget. That the BCFD was willing to take payments made it an even better bargain.

"Ooh. We should call Cliff." She reached for the phone.

Will propped his elbow on the visitor chair armrest. This was apparently going to take a while.

While the mayor was preoccupied, Will said to Sam, "I'm going to the Paydirt. See if I can't hitch a ride with someone back to the ranch."

"What's the hurry?"

"I've got to finish work on the sleigh."

Another of his boss's acquisitions. Sam had intended to decorate it with lights and display it at the entrance to the Gold Nugget. Will had instead suggested they give rides to the guests. Where that idea came from, he wasn't sure, but now he was stuck with it. The sleigh was in reasonably good condition but needed a few repairs before being able to carry passengers.

"Luiz can help you when we get back," Sam said.

Will didn't just sit around doing nothing when he could be doing something.

He glanced out the mayor's office window. They'd woken up that morning to three inches of freshly fallen snow. Not enough for cross-country skiing—that required another foot at least. But more than enough of the white stuff to turn the town and the Gold Nugget into a winter wonderland.

The contest winners and their families had left the previous day, raving about what a fantastic time they'd had. The publicity hadn't exactly worked miracles, from what Will had heard. Still, the ranch had gotten a few new reservations, some of those for the week between Christmas and New Year's. Most for the coming spring.

Sam and the mayor were devising a new promotion, bigger and grander and, in their opinion, guaranteed to revitalize the town's still-flagging economy. The mayor had dubbed the event the Mega Weekend of Weddings.

The idea was to perform a hundred wedding ceremonies back to back over a single weekend, setting a town record. Valentine's Day was too soon to pull it off. They'd agreed on June 3, the town's anniversary and the start of the summer season. Plus, as the mayor was quick to point out, who didn't want a June wedding?

"Cliff can swing by in about fifteen minutes," she said, disconnecting from her call. "He's on rounds."

"How 'bout I take the pickup to the ranch, unload the grain and come back for you?" Will thought the suggestion made sense. And it would get him out of this meeting.

Sam shot him down. "Once Cliff gets here, we can talk about delivery of the fire engine and training. I want you in on that."

Will's boot tapped a beat on the carpet.

"Excuse me a minute." The mayor answered her ringing phone. As she listened, her mouth thinned. "I haven't heard from her. Call Cissy, see if she can cover." Hanging up, she faced Will and Sam. "Sorry about that. Problem at the bar."

"Everything okay?" Sam asked.

"One of my waitresses didn't show up for her shift, and we can't reach her. Her phone keeps going straight to voice mail."

Will knew without being told. "Miranda?"

"Yes." The mayor turned to him. "Do you by chance know where she is?"

"She had an appointment this morning." Before he'd left the Paydirt yesterday, she had mentioned her meeting with the loan officer. "I could go look for her." He pushed to his feet. "It's right down the road."

"Would you mind? We're waiting on Cliff anyway."

Will hurried the half block to the savings and loan. Inside, he asked a teller if Miranda was still here. The young man checked with the loan officer and reported that Miranda had left almost an hour earlier.

He didn't ask how the meeting went. His gut told him not well.

Outside, he headed toward the residential district where Miranda's house was located. The walk wasn't a long one. Shorter if he jogged.

Careful not to slip on the snow-covered sidewalks, he called Sam. "Miranda wasn't where I thought she might be. Tell the mayor I'm stopping by her place." Will all but broke into a run after hanging up.

He reached Miranda's street several minutes later, sweat soaking the shirt beneath his jacket despite the cold. He was almost to her house when his cell phone rang. Sam's number appeared on the display.

"Yeah," he huffed.

"Mayor Dempsey just heard from Miranda."

"Is she okay?"

"Apparently."

"Where is she?"

"The mayor didn't say."

Will stopped on the sidewalk in front of Harmony House. Bending over, he braced his free hand on his knee, catching his breath. "All right. I'm on my way back."

All at once he caught a flash of movement in the front window. Must be one of the residents. No, not unless Babs or Mrs. Litey had grown blond hair in the past few days.

"Wait," he said an instant before Sam hung up. "I might be a while longer. Start the meeting without me."

"Will? What's going on?"

"Call you later." He pocketed his cell phone, walked to the front door and knocked.

As she'd done so often, Miranda answered the door. Only this time, she'd obviously been crying.

"Oh, honey." He stepped inside and opened his arms.

Without any hesitation, she flew at him and broke into fresh tears.

After a moment, he led her to the couch and sat them both down. Crackers wandered over for a quick ear scratching and settled on the floor by their feet.

"What happened?" Will asked gently.

Between Miranda's soft sobs and the occasional hiccup, he had trouble understanding her. Eventually he gleaned enough of the story; her application to refinance had been turned down. And with Mr. Lexington's imminent departure, she was terrified of losing her house and business.

"Is there anything I can do to help?" He stroked her back, enjoying a little too much how good it felt when she leaned into him.

He'd missed these moments. Being close to a woman. Giving comfort. Providing that soft place for her to fall.

How long until he failed Miranda, just as he'd failed everyone else he ever cared about?

Suddenly the room became a vacuum, void of oxygen. His chest constricted, compressed beneath the force of a thick metal band.

Stop this, you hear me?

Miranda's voice resounded inside his head, calming him better than any mantra he'd previously tried. The room miraculously opened up as if fresh air was being blown in through a vent.

"I don't mean to be such an emotional wreck." Her voice, while thready, was steadier.

"It's okay. You're entitled." He looked around, suddenly realizing they were alone. "Where is everyone?"

"Nell took them to the general store so they could do some Christmas shopping. I think they're also stopping at the pharmacy." Miranda released a wobbly sigh. "I was scheduled to work at the Paydirt today, but I just couldn't go in. Maybe later."

"I know. Sam and I were in Mayor Dempsey's office when she got the call that you hadn't shown up."

She gazed at him, her lashes damp spikes. "So you drove here?"

"Actually, I walked." More like ran.

The corners of her mouth lifted in the tiniest of smiles. "Really?"

He removed his cowboy hat and wiped his still-damp brow. "It's farther than it looks."

"Why?"

"Sam drove from the ranch. I didn't want to take his truck."

"That's not why you walked. Why did you come here? You could have called."

"To check on you. At first no one knew where you were."

She nodded. "I told Mayor Dempsey I was sick. I owe her the truth. And an apology."

"She'll understand, I'm sure."

"I'd have taken *your* call." She snuggled deeper in the crook of his arm. "But I'm glad you came by instead. This is much nicer." She placed a hand on his leg.

The warmth of her fingers penetrated the fabric of his jeans. Desire, hot and hard, spread through him.

Will groaned. He'd made a career of suppressing his emotions. All kinds, good and bad. This one, however, was stronger than most.

She must have sensed his rising need—or seen the evidence he couldn't hide—for she turned into him and pressed her lips to the hollow beneath his jawline.

"Miranda." Her name had a desperate ring.

Then again, Will was desperate. To get away from her... and to cover every inch of her body with every inch of his.

His need was a fire. In another minute it would rage unchecked. And then would come the panic attack.

The thought was enough to galvanize him. "I should go."

"No. Please stay."

"If I don't leave now—"

"What, Will?" Her hand crept perilously close to where it had no business being. "We'll make love?"

"You're vulnerable right now."

As was he. She was getting closer by the second, worming her way into the places he diligently guarded.

"Damn straight I'm vulnerable. This hasn't exactly been my week."

"It wouldn't be right for me to take advantage of you."

He shifted, hoping she'd get the hint and move her hand. Instead, it crept ever closer to the danger zone.

Putting her mouth to his ear, she whispered, "What if I were to take advantage of you?"

WILL WAS ON his feet, grabbing his jacket off the arm of the couch. If he didn't leave right now, he wouldn't be responsible for what transpired next. "Your residents will be home soon."

"Not for hours. Besides…" Miranda also rose. Slowly. Her movements sensual and evocative. "We're going to my room upstairs. Nell's the only one capable of climbing the stairs, and she wouldn't dare. Not without paging me on the intercom first. And everyone thinks I'm at the Paydirt."

As much as he wanted Miranda, and, God help him, he wanted her in the worst way possible, he resisted. "This isn't a good idea."

"I disagree." She sauntered toward him. "It's the best idea I've had in a long time."

"I don't…"

"What?" She laughed, though there was no merriment in it. "Have pity sex with women?"

"No!"

"Trust me." She sobered. "I know you wouldn't do that."

Returning his jacket to the couch, she linked her arms around his neck and pressed her lips to his. Will's resolve crumbled. He kissed her like a starved man. Even the possibility of a panic attack wasn't enough of a threat to dissuade him.

"You care about me." She bit his lower lip and drew it between her teeth. "I can tell. You also want me. I need that. To be cared for and wanted." A trace of sadness appeared in her eyes. "And to forget."

"I've thought of taking you to bed since we met."

"Then do it."

"Not like this." He held her close and rested his chin on the top of her head. "If we ever make love, it won't be to forget. It'll be to create memories. Incredible ones."

She clung to him. "I'm hurting, Will. Make me feel better." She kissed him full on the mouth, her lips petal soft and tasting like nectar.

Every fiber of his being resisted, told him this was wrong. As usual, Miranda was impossible to refuse. She was all subtle curves, pliant limbs and sweet-smelling skin.

Will caved. To hell with the consequences.

Hauling her against him, he took her mouth with a ferocity unlike before, determined to drive her as crazy as she was driving him. Her response was equally explosive, equally fierce.

Her fingers tore at the snaps on his shirt, shoving it off his shoulders. When the material bunched at his elbows, he shed the shirt as fast as possible. So much for sanity returning.

It was hardly off before they were kissing again. Tugging at the hem of her sweater, he slid his hand beneath it, desperate to feel her naked skin. He found what he was seeking and it nearly knocked him to his knees. She wasn't wearing a bra. Nothing covered the gloriously silky expanse of her back except his palms, which skimmed the entire length.

A car engine roared to life somewhere outside, the sound penetrating his muddled brain. Nell and the residents weren't returning home, but they would eventually.

"We should probably stop while we still can."

Miranda, typically the talkative one, said nothing. She simply crossed the room to the hall. She didn't look back; she didn't need to. Will was right behind her.

The door leading to the attic squeaked when she opened it, the hinges crying out for oil. The stairs groaned under their feet, announcing their progress. There would be no sneaking in and out when the residents were here.

Will came to a halt, his hand on the polished wooden rail. He and Miranda had yet to make love and he was already contemplating the future. One that was, realistically, filled with uncertainty.

A familiar and unsettling sensation hovered at the fringes. He gripped the railing tightly. A sharp pain shot up his arm.

Stop this, you hear me? Her voice echoed inside his head again.

He raised his gaze. She waited for him on the landing. If he was going to turn back, this was his last chance. He took a step up the stairs toward her.

"Are you all right?" Miranda asked, smiling when he reached her.

Light from a circular window streamed in, illuminating the attic suite behind her just enough that Will could distinguish the outline of bedroom furniture.

"Yeah." He almost cringed at the rough quality of his voice. If she sent him back the way he'd come, he wouldn't blame her.

She retreated into the room, and he thought she was

going to do exactly that. Instead she lifted her sweater over her head. "Good. Because I'm through waiting."

At the sight of her bare breasts, Will's mind emptied of everything save her. Need overruled reason. Desire vanquished fear. He would not disappoint her.

She twirled just as he reached for her and started toward the bed. Will moved to the center of the room and watched as she unfastened her pants. She paused only long enough to shimmy out of them and discard the thick socks she'd been wearing.

He swore his heart stopped. In fact, he was convinced of it.

Miranda wore nothing but the sheerest, skimpiest thong panties. If he'd known the kind of underwear she favored, about the *lack* of underwear, he would have clammed up every time they were together.

At the bed, she stopped and drew back the colorful spread. Despite a slight chill to the room, Will doubted they'd need any covering. He was plenty hot enough to keep them both warm.

She faced him, the sadness gone from her eyes. "You going to stand there all day, cowboy?"

The idea was appealing. She was certainly something to look at. More appealing, however, was the idea of holding her in his arms, burying himself deep inside her.

Reclining onto the bed, she opened her arms. He went to her, not yet ready to shed his jeans and boots, and she pulled him down onto the mattress. Will pinned her beneath him. Bracing his elbows on either side of her, he stared into her face.

"What?" she asked, suddenly self-conscious.

"You're beautiful."

Her cheeks flushed an appealing pink. "You're only saying that because I'm nearly naked and underneath you."

He brushed a lock of hair from her forehead. She was

making light of the situation; he understood that. Emotions were on the line. The risk of being hurt existed. Considering his track record, it was practically a given.

But she was too important for him to take what was about to occur between them casually.

"I'm saying that because you are. Inside and out. I've never met anyone like you, Miranda, and that isn't a line. You're a wonderful, generous, giving person. I wish I could promise you that I won't let you down. I can only promise you that I'll try my best not to."

"Why, Will Dessaro, I do believe that's the longest speech I've ever heard you make."

"You may be right."

She tenderly caressed his cheek. "I know this isn't easy for you. Please don't worry. If you start to struggle, we can always—"

He cut her off with a kiss. Will knew more than most that there was a time for words and a time for action. Lying in bed with Miranda in his arms was definitely a time for action.

Rolling onto his back, he pulled her with him, settling her on top of him so that their positions were reversed. With one arm around her waist and the other cupping her buttocks, he pressed his erection firmly into her tummy.

She closed her eyes. "Mmm…nice."

He couldn't wait to—

Will went still. It was unusual for him to get so carried away that he forgot about protection.

"What?"

"We, uh…" Damn, he just needed to say it. "Condoms. I don't have one. I wasn't planning for this."

"No worries." Miranda slid herself off him, hopped off the bed and padded to the dresser in the corner. Opening the bottom drawer, she dug around and removed a small box.

Will was speechless, even for him. She kept a box of condoms in her dresser?

"It's not what you think." She set the box on the night-stand, within easy reach. "I bought these for Babs."

"Babs?" He was positive he'd heard wrong.

"Technically, for her and Arthur."

He tried envisioning the elderly couple doing the deed. "Babs and Arthur..." He couldn't finish. It was all too much.

"I don't ask." Miranda climbed back into the bed and nestled beside Will. "What they do when they're alone is their private business. But people of any age need to prac-tice safe sex."

Will wasn't sure if he'd ever get the image of Babs and Arthur out of his mind. Then Miranda reached for his belt buckle and his attention snapped back to her.

Struggling with the snap on his jeans, she made a face. "These have to go."

He obliged her. The rest of his clothes weren't far be-hind. Miranda sighed approvingly as she slid Will's boxer briefs over his hips and down his legs. Grinning wickedly, she reached for his erection, filling her hands with it and stroking gently. Every one of his muscles tensed to the point of snapping.

One minute was the most he could endure, and he nudged her hands away.

"I wasn't done," she complained with a sexy pout.

Grabbing a condom off the nightstand, he put it on with shaking fingers. Then he eased her onto her back. "And I've only just begun."

Will covered her breasts, kneading and plying them, then brought the closest one to his mouth. The nipple was pert and firm and sweeter than rock candy. Miranda watched him lick and suckle while murmuring her approval.

Her face, always so readable, displayed everything she

was feeling. Delight. Excitement. Anticipation. Arousal. Never the least bit shy, she raised her hips, issuing a provocative invitation that set his blood on fire.

Enough was enough. Will slipped a thumb into the elastic leg band of her thong and shoved it aside.

"Wait," she cooed, her sultry voice sliding over him. "Let me." She wriggled out of the thong in a seductive dance that drove him right to the edge.

With the barrier effectively removed, he entered her with his fingers. She was damp and ready for him.

"Oh, my." She threw her head back onto the pillow, a moan escaping.

"Tell me what you like."

She did, by moving her body, guiding his hand and whispering words of encouragement. Will concentrated on her, which wasn't easy. His own need was demanding equal time.

"No more." She shifted away.

"Did I hurt you?" And here he'd thought she was close to climaxing.

"Not at all." She parted her legs, wriggled seductively. "I want you inside me when I come."

Will nearly lost it, but not before he entered her with a single thrust. Stars exploded behind his eyelids. She was tight and slick and warm and all his. He pushed deeper, then deeper still.

Her legs circled his middle and she rose up to meet him, taking all of him and giving more in return.

Exercising self-control he didn't know he possessed, he held back. It was torture. It was also heaven. He felt good. She felt great.

He changed the angle of his penetration, increased the rhythm. It was enough. Her shattering climax sent Will sailing to find his own release. They clung to each other until their tremors subsided.

He didn't want to move. Ever. Didn't want to leave Miranda or this bed. This house.

She melted into the mattress. "That was... Wow."

He couldn't agree more.

They curled together under the covers, not satisfied until their bodies were touching from head to toe. Content at last, they lay quietly, letting their beating hearts do the talking.

Will's chest constricting brought the moment to an end. He increased his hold on Miranda and waited.

Not a panic attack. This, he realized, was what it was like to fall for someone.

Fall harder, he corrected himself. He'd been under Miranda's spell since the day he had first seen her.

Chapter Eleven

Miranda propped herself up on one elbow and studied Will. He'd fallen into a light sleep soon after they'd made love. She shouldn't be surprised—he'd rigorously maintained control, not wavering for one second. It had to be draining.

He was even more gorgeous in slumber, and that was saying a lot because he was totally gorgeous awake. The lines bracketing his mouth and creasing his brow had relaxed, leaving smooth tanned skin in its place. She longed to run her fingertips over the contours of his face but refrained, afraid she might disturb him.

Sighing, she snuggled next to him. Her contentment was short-lived. Almost instantly she recalled her wretched morning. Will's incredible lovemaking—and it was incredible—had only temporarily set her mind free.

The savings and loan had turned her down flat. Mr. Lexington was leaving.

Miranda had no idea what to do. Anything short of finding new residents, full- or part-time, was simply delaying the inevitable.

Arthur came immediately to mind. She frowned at the recollection of her chance meeting with his daughter and son-in-law the other day. It was unfair and selfish of them, expecting her to accommodate Arthur all day, nearly every day, let him eat her food and watch her TV and not compensate her.

What if she just presented them with a bill?

That wouldn't be nice. And what if they put an end to Arthur's visits? Babs would be desolate.

Miranda supposed she could speak to Arthur directly. Not to ask him for compensation. Good heavens, she wouldn't dream of doing that. He might, however, be interested in moving in. Enough to override his daughter's objections.

She'd do it, Miranda decided. Drop a hint anyway. What could it hurt?

There was also the bulletin board at the community center. She'd advertised there before. For live-in residents, not adult day care. She could post notices at Sweetheart's three churches, too.

Yesterday Miranda had run into Wanda at the drugstore. The grade-school teacher had mentioned receiving government assistance for her home and gave Miranda the contact info. The program was for residents, however, not businesses. Still, it was worth checking into, seeing as Miranda ran her business out of her home.

Will stirred, putting an end to her mental meanderings. She wriggled closer and wrapped a leg around his. This was nice, lying beside a warm male body. She could get used to it.

What might the future hold for them? Miranda hadn't dated much since opening Harmony House. What man in his right mind got involved with a woman who lived with four senior citizens?

Something told her Will was different. He didn't visit her just because Mrs. Litey reminded him of his grandmother. He liked her residents. Kids, too. It was everyone else he kept at a distance.

Except for her. She'd managed to breach his defenses, but it hadn't been easy. So worth it, however.

She started at the sudden sound of an unfamiliar cell

phone chiming. It came from the floor. More specifically, Will's jeans.

He jackknifed to a sitting position, blinking sleep from his eyes. "Where's my phone?"

"It's over there, I think."

He swung his feet onto the floor and bent down to retrieve his jeans. The phone was still ringing when he pulled it out of the back pocket.

"Yeah, Sam." He sent Miranda a bashful look she found quite endearing, as if his boss could see through the phone and knew what they'd done. "I got distracted...She's fine," he added after a pause. "I'll tell you later."

Miranda sat up and hugged Will from behind, doing her dead level best to distract him. Her efforts had the desired effect.

"How'd the meeting go? Sorry I missed it." Will cleared his throat. "I can do that."

She bit his shoulder as her hand crept down his belly.

"Right, I'll just..." He covered a groan with another throat clearing. "Go ahead. I'll catch a ride back to the ranch. I'm sure." He closed his eyes and leaned into her as she found him and began stroking. "Gotta go."

Miranda could hear Sam still talking as Will disconnected the phone. Unable to help herself, she laughed. Will did, too.

She went still, realizing she hadn't heard him laugh before and marveling at the rich timbre. Before she quite knew what was happening, he flipped her onto her back and rolled on top of her, staring at her with a lightness in his eyes that was also new.

She threaded her fingers into his hair and brought his mouth to hers. "I like hearing you laugh. You should do it more often."

"Invite me up here and I will."

"What are you doing tomorrow?" She flashed him a wicked grin.

That was all it took. Their second joining was fast and as explosive as the first. Will held on to her when it was over as though she was the most precious thing in the world. Miranda went all fluttery inside.

They might have lain there indefinitely—wouldn't that be lovely?—but muffled noises from below traveled up the stairway.

"Darn." She feigned alarm. "I think we just got busted."

Will's alarm, on the other hand, was genuine. He swore under his breath and threw back the covers. "Is there another way out of here?"

"You are not climbing down the rain gutter." She followed him out of bed and retrieved her clothes, which were strewn across the floor.

"I could go through the heating vent to the garage."

"We haven't done anything wrong." She couldn't believe how irritated she was by his guilt.

"Miranda." He was beside her in an instant, half dressed and looking sexier than ever. "This was more than right. It was meant to be."

Her heart sang. What a perfect thing to say.

"I'm just worried about you and your reputation." He dropped a kiss on her cheek. "I don't want your residents and Nell thinking less of you. Or their families, if they mention anything. It could hurt your business."

"Need I remind you why I purchased the condoms? Babs and Arthur can be trusted to stay quiet. Mrs. Litey will be thrilled to see you and probably not notice that you came from upstairs. I'd be surprised if Himey paid any attention. And Mr. Lexington is leaving this weekend. Who cares what he or his son thinks?"

"What about Nell? She's your employee."

"Seriously? She'll find the whole thing hilarious. It'll be all right," she affirmed when he remained skeptical.

"If you say so." He kissed her again before leaving her alone so they both could finish dressing. Moments later, the intercom went off, the shrill buzzing loud enough to wake Miranda from the soundest of sleeps if necessary.

She went over to the wall and depressed the button. "Yes."

"You *are* up there." Nell's deep voice boomed from the intercom. "The Paydirt called a while ago. We were in the middle of shopping. For personal necessities." She stressed the word *personal*. "You know how that goes. By the time I called them back, they said they'd found you."

"Sorry about that. Be down in a sec."

"Okay. Maybe then you can tell us why Will's hat, jacket and shirt are in the front room. Babs thought maybe he forgot them in his haste." There was a pause during which Miranda swore Nell silenced a giggle.

Will grimaced.

Miranda motioned for him to relax. Facing everyone downstairs wouldn't be easy. Will, however, was good at keeping a straight face. As long as the stress didn't trigger a panic attack.

"Give me a minute." She released the intercom button and faced him. "We probably should have skipped... You know, that second time. Then we wouldn't be forced to take the walk of shame."

He captured her hand as they started toward the stairs. "I wouldn't have skipped 'you know' for anything."

Neither would she.

Instead of the entire household waiting for them at the base of the stairs as she'd expected, they were busy elsewhere. In fact, the front room was completely empty except for Crackers. At the sight of Will, the terrier trotted over.

Nell was with Babs, helping her sort and stow her various purchases. Mrs. Litey had retired to her room. Himey was poking through the refrigerator contents, on the hunt for a snack. Mr. Lexington was, of course, napping. She'd miss him when he was gone.

At once she was filled with sorrow. Will, astute as always, squeezed her fingers.

"I best get going." He retrieved his jacket, shirt and hat, which had been placed in a neat stack on the couch, and slipped on his shirt.

She walked him to the door, glad they were alone. "Will I see you tomorrow?" She hated that her voice rose at the end.

"Absolutely. I'll call you. Find out when's a good time."

"Or you can call…just to talk." She gazed at him shyly.

"I will." His smile warmed her. "If there's anything I can do to help with your problem, let me know."

"I can't imagine there is, but I'll keep the offer in mind. I actually have a few ideas I'm tossing around." She glanced over her shoulder. They were still alone. "Not sure they'll work, but I've got to stay positive."

She would, too.

Not daring to do more than rest her hand on his arm, she said, "Bye."

The next thing she knew, she was in his arms, his mouth planted firmly on hers. The kiss was swift but thorough.

"My goodness!" was all she could muster when he set her aside.

"See you later, honey." He plunked his hat on his head and left.

Honey? Miranda was thrilled at the easy way the endearment had rolled off his tongue. She closed the door and leaned her back against it. Shutting her eyes, she relived the past two hours, cherishing every moment. Tomorrow couldn't come fast enough. Maybe he wouldn't be able to wait and would call her tonight.

The shuffle of footsteps roused her. She really needed to get some work done. Opening her eyes, she pushed off the door and stopped suddenly.

Five pairs of eyes were staring at her. Six if she counted Crackers. When had everyone wandered into the front room?

Great. Had they seen her and Will kissing?

Before she could stammer an excuse, Mrs. Litey asked, "Lois, was that Joseph? When did you two start seeing each other?"

Nell exploded in a raucous belly laugh.

WILL STOOD BACK and inspected his craftsmanship. The old sleigh was ready for its maiden voyage. Well, not its first outing ever but its first one in possibly four decades.

He'd been laboring over the sleigh for an entire week, in between leading cross-country ski excursions and one trail ride up to the Windfall Claim site.

The skiers were stout individuals who had been eager to go out again the next day. The horse riders hadn't endured the cold well and had found other, less arduous, activities to entertain themselves, mostly in town. With more snow in the forecast, Will was certain he'd led his last trail ride till next spring.

Maybe on his maiden voyage with the sleigh he'd go to Miranda's place. Convince her to join him. Heck, he'd give all the residents a ride. Babs and Himey would love it. Arthur, too, who'd probably be there. Mrs. Litey, maybe not so much. He'd have to explain how Joseph had learned to drive a sleigh.

Just Miranda, then. The two of them cuddled together on the seat, keeping warm with a blanket and each other. That was, if the sleigh made it. The hard asphalt could damage the metal runners if the snow and ice weren't packed solidly enough. He really should drive the sleigh around the ranch first.

Reservations at the Gold Nugget had picked up recently. Thanks to school holidays, they were booked almost to capacity for the first time since the ranch opened. Christmas next week was going to be a merry event, what with dinner being served in the main house and a surprise visit from Santa Claus in the works. Sam was also hosting a kid-friendly New Year's Eve party.

He'd asked Will to give sleigh rides after Christmas dinner. He'd also invited Will to eat with his family and the guests, which Will had declined. Sam hadn't asked for a reason, and Will didn't volunteer one. His boss likely guessed that Will would be dining at Harmony House with Miranda, Nell and the three remaining residents.

Who knew how long her elder-care business would stay afloat? The holidays were a lousy time to look for new residents. Her attempts at advertising had yet to yield any results.

Will had spent the previous weekend helping Mr. Lexington's son move the old man out. It had been a sad and trying occasion for everyone. Mr. Lexington had objected vehemently to the move, arguing heatedly and then, at the end, crying like a baby. Miranda and Babs had cried, too. Mrs. Litey completely retreated into the past, and Himey hid in his room.

When the time came for Mr. Lexington to leave, they'd had to pry Crackers from his arms when he had refused to part with the dog.

Miranda handled the move well until Mr. Lexington's son drove away. Then she fell apart. Will had done what he could to console her. Eventually she'd pulled herself together, staying strong for her remaining residents. The strain was beginning to show on her face, however, in the form of dark circles under her eyes and a pale complexion.

If he thought she'd take his money, he'd give her all he could spare. But she'd refuse. She'd already turned her parents down.

A sleigh ride might cheer her up. At the very least get her out of the house and doing something else besides working at the Paydirt. He could pick her up when she finished her shift later today for a moonlight ride. Of course, if he picked her up, everyone would know they were seeing each other.

Will had found himself caring less and less what other people thought of him. It was an interesting change. A permanent one, he hoped.

At the sound of bells, he raised his head. Cruze, who'd been snoozing nearby, jumped to his feet, tail wagging.

Sam was crossing the open area in front of the barn, picking his way over the freshly plowed snow.

"Thought you might want to use these," Sam said when he neared.

"Where'd you find them?" Will took the jingle bells from Sam and examined them.

A dozen brass bells had been fastened to a leather strap. At the end of the strap was a clasp, enabling it to be attached to the horse's harness. The bells—Will was sure they were antique—made a pleasant sound when shaken.

"Annie found them," Sam answered. "Borrowed them, actually. From the Sweetheart Memorial."

Sam's wife was on the committee that ran the memorial. The recently constructed museum housed all manner of memorabilia from before the fire that had ravaged the town last July.

"I think they're from the old Overbeck place."

Will laid the jingle bells next to the toolbox. "The guests will like them."

"Yeah," Sam agreed. "Over the river and through the woods."

"Does this mean I have to sing Christmas carols while I'm driving?"

"That's something I'd want to see." His boss chuckled as he walked around the sleigh, giving it a thorough once-over. "Looks as if you're ready for a test drive."

"I was just thinking the same thing myself. Want to go? I cleaned the harness yesterday."

"Which horse are you using?"

"Sugar Pie. I'm not in the mood for a rodeo."

The old draft mare was dependable and complacent. Trustworthy enough to carry a three-year-old through an earthquake. Plus she had driving experience, having once been part of a team.

"Good choice." Sam ran a gloved hand along the sleigh's wooden side, pausing briefly where Will had patched a hole. "But I think your first passenger should be Miranda, seeing as you two are going out these days."

Will's response was to raise his brows.

"Your truck's been parked in front of her house four nights in a row. Irma noticed and mentioned it."

Irma was head housekeeper at the ranch. Will had forgotten she lived on the same street as Miranda.

"Hey, don't be mad," Sam said when Will returned to cleaning the sleigh. "I'm glad you're seeing her. I told you that before."

"I'm not mad." Will wasn't. He'd just kept to himself for so long, discussing the personal aspects of his life didn't come easy.

Maybe he should give it a try. He could use a sounding board.

"You finished for the day?" Will asked.

"Just about. What do you have in mind?"

"Thought maybe I'd buy you a beer at the Paydirt."

"A special occasion?"

"Not really."

But it was, and Sam must have figured it out for he readily agreed.

Together they pushed the sleigh back into the empty stall where Will had been storing it. Moony, the pony in the neighboring stall, squealed and kick at the loud ruckus they created.

A half hour later Will and Sam were seated at a table, Miranda taking their order. She gave Will's shoulder the lightest of squeezes before leaving to fetch their beers. Not so much that anyone would think twice. Sam obviously saw it. He smiled and toasted Miranda when the beers arrived.

"There's something I've been wanting to tell you," Will said once she left to wait on another customer.

"What's that?"

Will talked, then. It was the longest and most revealing conversation he'd had in years. His entire story poured out, from the accident that had caused his parents' deaths but spared him to how he'd come to live in Sweetheart. He also told Sam about his inability to leave town, apologizing for not accepting the council's offer to pay for EMT training.

Sam said nothing. Proving what a good friend he was, he simply listened intently while drinking his beer. When Will was done, he leaned back in his chair and stretched out his legs.

"Well, the offer still stands," he said. "If things change."

Will shook his head. "I doubt that will happen."

"Who knows? You've made a lot of progress recently. You're seeing Miranda, interacting with people on a personal level, talking more. Maybe you should try leaving town again."

Sam's point was worth considering.

They returned to the ranch as the sun was setting. Will fetched Cruze, who'd been waiting in the barn, and they both jumped into his truck. Will intended to head for home and kill time until Miranda was off work. Instead he drove to the edge of town. Sam was right. Will had made significant progress, and he was convinced he could make it past the boundary with no problem.

He continued to remain optimistic until he was an eighth of a mile beyond the Welcome to Sweetheart sign and was forced to suddenly pull off the road and bail out.

If he hadn't, he would have heaved all over his truck instead of on a snowbank.

Chapter Twelve

Miranda fell to her knees on the rug by her bed, her cell phone jammed to her ear. She'd gone to her suite when Mrs. Litey's brother had called, for a bit of privacy. *Please, God. This couldn't be happening again. Not so soon.* It had only been a week since Mr. Lexington's son had moved him away.

"I hope you understand," Reverend Donahue said, compassion softening his voice but not the impact of the news he'd delivered. "I can't tell you how much I appreciate everything you've done for my sister. Considering how difficult she can be, I'm lucky you've taken care of her this long."

"She's no trouble." Miranda rested her forehead against the mattress.

"I'm thinking of coming for her on the Monday after New Year's," the reverend went on. "Don't want to cause you any inconvenience over the holidays."

Inconvenience? The man had just destroyed what was left of her business and possibly taken her home from her. How would she go on with only two residents left?

She couldn't. Even if she laid off Nell, the income from Babs and Himey wasn't enough to cover even half her expenses.

Miranda's spirit crumbled like a sand castle consumed by the rising tide. She bit back a sob. It wouldn't do to have

Reverend Donahue hear her crying. He was so excited about the prospect of reuniting with his sister. A sister who had improved considerably over the past few months, enough that he felt capable enough caring for her.

"What you've accomplished with her is nothing short of a miracle," he said.

"I can't take the credit. Will Dessaro is responsible."

"The man she believes to be her late son?"

"Yes. He's wonderful with her." A thought struck Miranda, and she sat straighter. It was grasping at straws, but she had nothing to lose. "Your sister's going to miss him terribly if you take her to live in Carson City."

"I realize that, and I wish things were different. If I hadn't so recently retired from the ministry, I'd be content for her to remain with you. Now that I have more time, I intend to dedicate myself to her. She helped put me through college. I wouldn't have become a minister without her."

"Caring for someone with Alzheimer's is more work than you realize. Without Will, she could regress." Another desperate attempt to dissuade him. Unfortunately, he was having none of it.

"I'm prepared. I'll need something to keep my mind and body occupied. Retiring hasn't been easy for me. I like being busy. Of course I'll pay you for the entire month of January."

Like Mr. Lexington's son, the reverend wasn't going to give her the full thirty-days' notice. Miranda didn't call him on it. Why bother when her home and business were a fast-sinking ship? Another week's income wouldn't save either of them.

How could this be happening? She'd worked so hard, sacrificed so much, done everything right to build Harmony House from the ground up. Then the fire had struck, causing a mass exodus of people from Sweetheart.

"I'll call later in the week once I've finalized the arrangements," Reverend Donahue said. "And if you'd be kind enough to remind her daily after that, I'd appreciate it. I told her when we talked earlier, but she won't remember."

"Certainly, I'll remind her."

"Do you suppose there's any chance this Will Dessaro would be willing to be there? It might make Leonora easier to handle."

"I can ask him. I'm sure he wants to say goodbye. He's very fond of your sister."

"I'll gladly reimburse him for his trouble."

She answered on Will's behalf, certain he wouldn't object. "Will wouldn't take any money. Not for moving your sister."

"He sounds like a fine young man."

The reverend couldn't have spoken truer words. Miranda was lucky to have fallen for such a good guy.

And she had fallen for him. Thoroughly. He would be devastated to hear about Mrs. Litey. Both because he'd miss her and for Miranda, knowing what a negative impact it was going to have on her business.

"I'll let you go, Reverend." Miranda sniffed. She wasn't sure how much longer she could hang on.

"I wish you the best, my dear. God bless you."

She was going to need all the blessings she could get if she had any hope of surviving this blow.

Miranda allowed herself a few minutes before pulling herself together. After freshening up in the small bathroom, she headed downstairs.

As if it mattered now. With only Babs and Himey left, there would be little need for thick walls and distance. Both were hard of hearing.

She felt as if she carried a thousand-pound backpack down the stairs. If not for the railing, she'd pitch forward and tumble to the bottom.

"What's wrong?" Arthur asked the moment she stepped into the front room.

Nell wasn't here today, having taken the day off. Thank goodness. She'd be harder to fool than Arthur.

"Nothing. Just tired."

"You look as if you just lost your best friend." He came over to her and returned the portable transmitter she'd entrusted him with.

Miranda didn't wish to leave her residents alone, even for a few minutes. They each wore a transmitter which, when activated, would sound an alarm over the intercom system as well as alert the monitoring company to call 9-1-1. On impulse she'd left one with Arthur, too, before going upstairs.

"Thank you." She pocketed the transmitter, hoping he didn't notice she'd ignored his comment.

He trailed her into the kitchen. Miranda ground her teeth. She really didn't want company right this minute.

"I'm going to start paying you," he said.

"What?" She grabbed a tissue from the box on the counter and dabbed her nose.

"My daughter told me you posted ads for adult day care on the bulletin boards at the community center and the First Community Church."

"Yes, but I didn't intend for you to—" Miranda stopped herself. Hadn't she hinted at him just a few days ago about compensating her?

"I've been freeloading too long. Time I pitched in."

"Thank you, Arthur." She was touched. Truly. But to be completely honest, it was too little, too late. Whatever amount he paid wouldn't make up for the residents she'd lost. "That won't be necessary."

"I insist." He stood taller. "I pay my way."

"All right." On impulse, she kissed his cheek. Compensating her was clearly important to him. And she had fed him a lot of meals since he and Babs had started seeing each other.

He smiled and touched his cheek where she'd kissed it. "My, my! You won't be telling Babs about that, will you? She's a mite jealous."

"Better get back to her before she becomes suspicious."

He did, leaving Miranda with the solitude she craved.

It was still too early to start dinner, so she fussed in the kitchen, rearranging cabinets and drawers and the pantry shelves. The busywork didn't take her mind off her woes.

At one point Miranda hugged herself, an arrow of fear piercing her. Her life was collapsing around her, and she was helpless to stop it.

"Miranda, look!" Himey called from the front room.

"You need to see this," Arthur seconded.

She wiped at her cheeks, not really surprised to find them damp, and hurried from the kitchen to see what was causing the excitement. In the middle of the room, she came to a sudden stop and stared out the window.

Will was disembarking from a bright red horse-drawn sleigh. As she watched, he tethered the horse to the corner post of her neighbor's fence. A light snow flurry had started at some point when she was in the kitchen and fell like powder. The scene could have come straight from the pages of a calendar or out of a storybook.

"Oh, Will," she muttered, her fingers clutching the fabric at her throat.

Another time she would have been utterly charmed. As it was, her worries about her home and business cast a dark pall on everything.

A moment later, he knocked at the door. Forcing a smile, Miranda let him in.

"What's this?" she asked. In the distance the horse bobbed her head, and a merry melody drifted toward them on the wind. "Are those jingle bells?"

Will grinned like a kid on Christmas morning. "Get your coat. We're going on a ride."

"Nell's off work today. I can't leave my residents alone."

"We'll take them with us. There's room for six in the sleigh. If we sit close."

"I don't think Mrs. Litey will want to leave the house." Speaking the woman's name only served to remind Miranda that she would have one less resident in a matter of weeks.

"Hey, are you okay?"

Her reply was interrupted by Arthur.

"I haven't been on a sleigh ride in decades." He pushed Babs's wheelchair closer to the window. "You want to go, darling?"

"Can we?" She fidgeted excitedly in her wheelchair.

Himey was equally enthusiastic and came up behind Miranda, squeezing past her to view the sleigh. "Don't see sleighs like these around much anymore. My dad had one when we were young'uns."

Miranda didn't want to go. She was neither jolly nor merry. The pressure, however, was coming at her from all sides. Will, Arthur, Babs, Himey. Her chest hurt. Breathing was increasingly difficult and her temples throbbed.

"Maybe tomorrow," she said.

Arthur, Babs and Himey looked stricken.

Miranda didn't like herself in that moment. She should put her personal woes aside and let Will take them all on a ride. Only she couldn't make her mouth operate properly or her feet move from where they were glued to the floor.

She wasn't the only casualty in this situation. Poor Babs and Himey had no one nearby to take them in. Without her, they could end up homeless.

"Miranda?" Will studied her face.

She felt her skin heat under his gaze. "I can't. I won't," she practically shouted. "No sleigh ride."

"Okay. We'll go another day."

He placed a hand on her shoulder. The gesture should have consoled her. Instead his hand felt like a boulder, crushing her beneath it. Another minute and she was going to die. Already colors bloomed behind her closed eyelids.

"Wh-what's wrong? I c-can't breathe," she stammered.

"Hold on, honey. I've got you."

Will supported her with an arm around her waist and murmured calming words. Hadn't she done the same things to him when he'd had a panic attack?

Oh, God! A panic attack. She was having one of her own, and it was awful.

Her last thought as she surrendered to the attack was how did Will survive these?

"HERE, PUT THIS around you." Will spread a blanket across Miranda's lap.

She was instantly warmer and slightly more in control. She wasn't, however, less scared.

"I'm not sure what came over me," she said, still mortified by her breakdown.

His arm circled her shoulder and he drew her snug against him. Someone must have given her a coat before she came outside and joined Will in the sleigh, but Miranda didn't remember who. She looked up. The horse was still tethered to the post. Apparently they weren't going on a ride, just sitting here.

"Something has you rattled," he said.

That was an understatement.

"Want to talk about it?"

Miranda glanced at the house. "I should probably get back inside. Nell's not working today."

"I think everyone will be okay for a few minutes. Besides, you can see them from here."

He was right. Three faces were peering out the window, watching her and Will. Only Babs was missing. She probably couldn't maneuver her wheelchair to the window.

"They must think I've lost it."

"They're worried about you." Will kissed her brow. "Like me."

She owed him an explanation. "I got a call from Reverend Donahue, Mrs. Litey's brother. He retired a few months ago. Now that he has more time, and now that Mrs. Litey is doing better, he wants to take care of her."

"Not in Sweetheart, I take it."

"Carson City. He's coming for her the Monday after New Year's." She rubbed her bare hands together, vaguely recalling that Crackers had chewed her last pair of gloves.

Crackers! Oh, no. What would happen to her little dog? She started shaking again.

Will covered her hands with his. "Oh, honey, I'm sorry."

His sympathy was sweet and kind. It also triggered a fresh wave of tears. "These things happen. It comes with running a business." But did it have to come all at once?

"It's my fault."

That dried her tears. "What are you saying?"

"If I hadn't started visiting Mrs. Litey, she wouldn't have improved."

"Don't even think that way. What you did for her is wonderful. I'd rather she improve and go live with her brother than remain the way she was, miserable and making everyone around her miserable." She could tell from his expression that he didn't believe her. "Really, Will, it's fine. The fire is to blame, not you."

"What are your plans?" he asked after a moment.

"I don't have any yet." She pressed her hands to her mouth. "Other than not losing my house."

"We won't let that happen."

She noticed his use of the plural. That was his guilt talking. "This isn't your problem. It's mine."

"I'll help you any way I can."

"Including teaching me to cope with panic attacks?" She shook her head, the irony not lost on her. Last week, she'd been the one teaching him. "I can't believe that happened."

"It's probably a one-time reaction to stress. I wouldn't worry just yet."

As a nurse, she knew that. Even so, she felt no better.

"I have to make a decision. Soon. My January payment is due in ten days and I don't have the money for it." Her temples pounded. A reaction to her momentary stress incident. Thinking was impossible.

"Why don't I talk to Sam's wife? Or you can."

"About what?"

"She and her mother researched federal grants after their inn burned. They could maybe point you in the right direction."

"Not sure that will do any good. Wanda from the grade school told me about an assistance program, and it turned out to be a dead end."

"Still might be worth talking to Annie."

"I don't disagree, but applying for and receiving a grant will require weeks, if not months. I don't have that kind of time."

"You could talk to the bank again. They may have other options."

"Like foreclosure? No, thank you." She released a tired sigh. "I suppose I could take my folks up on their offer."

"You're lucky they support you."

"I hate being the adult child who keeps running to their parents for a loan. Besides, the most they could afford to lend me would only get me through another month. With Arthur's help, I might last six weeks."

"Arthur?"

"He volunteered to chip in."

"He should."

Miranda glanced at the window again. There were four faces now. Babs had succeeded in joining the group and was staring out from the lower corner.

Despite the distance, she could discern the concern and curiosity on their faces. "Arthur can't pay me enough to keep me afloat. Only full-time residents will do that." She curled into a ball, burying her face in the blanket. "I hate this. Hate it, hate it."

Will gave her a moment, stroking her back, and then asked, "What about taking a break from elder care and working full-time at the Paydirt? Just temporarily."

Right, temporarily. Like Cissy. She was supposedly waitressing just until she landed a job as an accountant, the field in which she'd obtained her degree. Except she'd been at the Paydirt almost three years now.

Miranda refused to follow in her coworker's footsteps.

"The mayor hired me mostly as a favor. She doesn't need another full-time employee." She groaned out of anger and frustration. "I love being a nurse. This is so unfair."

"What about the clinic in town?"

She pondered Will's suggestion. "I could ask, but I doubt they're hiring. I'm there every week. Sometimes twice a week. I'd have heard about a job opening."

"Doesn't hurt to ask."

"I could always move to Reno. Work at the hospital. I left on good terms."

"You'd do that?" Will's arm increased its hold, as if she was leaving that second.

"It would be my very last choice. Believe me."

"What would you do with your house if you moved?"

"Rent it, maybe. There's still a housing shortage in Sweetheart since the fire. I'd have takers." At the anguish in his eyes, she added, "But I'm not leaving. How could I, when we just found each other?"

He smiled at her, the tension so visible earlier having

lessened. "Then we'll just have to find you another resident."

She smiled in return, though it was wobbly at best. One resident wouldn't cut it. She needed nothing less than a full house.

"Speaking of residents, I should tell Babs and Himey to start looking for another place to live."

"Want some moral support?"

"You'd come in with me?"

"Sure."

"What about the horse?"

"She'll be fine tied to the post. For a while."

Will climbed down from the sleigh first and then assisted Miranda. They walked hand in hand to the door. Inside, she delivered the news about Harmony House's potential closing. As expected, everyone was devastated, except Mrs. Litey, who thought the Gold Nugget was closing and started ranting and raving.

The reverend was going to have his work cut out for him.

When Will tried to reason with her, she glared at him as if he were a complete stranger and snipped, "Young man, do I know you? What do you want with me?"

Miranda braced herself for what promised to be a terrible next two weeks.

Chapter Thirteen

Miranda's days, it seemed, were destined to go from bad to worse. While the entire town of Sweetheart was caught up in celebrating Christmas this Saturday, she was fighting a losing battle to save her home and business.

Annie Wyler had provided Miranda with several numbers to call for federal and state grants. Unfortunately, the waiting lists were long, compounded by delays due to the holidays. Another useless dead end.

In the meantime, Reverend Donahue had called twice, speaking to Mrs. Litey and then to Miranda about the move. Himey wandered from room to room as if lost, and Babs had sunk into a deep depression that even Arthur's loyalty and constant attention couldn't dispel.

Babs's son had reluctantly agreed to take her into his small and already crowded home near Lake Tahoe. He really didn't want to, and Babs dreaded going, convinced she'd never see Arthur again.

Sadly, Miranda thought that might be true. Arthur wasn't capable of making the trip on his own, and his daughter was "too busy" to drive him there.

Not nice. Miranda instantly scolded herself for being petty. Her situation was no more Arthur's daughter's fault than Will's. Fate had simply dealt her a very crummy hand.

Nell, for her part, was being a saint. She'd agreed to stay to the bitter end, without pay if it came to that. Miranda refused to take advantage of her friend and employee. Nell, however, insisted. They'd discussed the daunting task of packing up the residents' rooms. Miranda didn't have the heart to start yet.

Heading upstairs to her suite, she sat on the edge of her bed, gathered her courage and called Mr. Carter at Northern Nevada Savings and Loan.

"Hi, Miranda," he greeted her, his tone warm.

He might not be so nice to her when he learned the reason for her call. "Mr. Carter, I don't suppose there's been any change in policy recently. I could really use that lower mortgage payment."

"I'm sorry, no. You'd be the first person I'd call if there was."

She swallowed the large and painful lump lodged in her throat. "Then I guess I need to talk to you about letting the mortgage go into foreclosure."

The silence that followed lasted several seconds. "Are you sure? Foreclosure isn't a step you want to take if you can avoid it."

"I'm at my wit's end," she said hoarsely. "I've scoured Sweetheart from top to bottom. There are no new residents to be found."

"That's one of the disadvantages of living in a small town."

"The economy isn't doing me any favors. People are choosing to care for their elderly family members at home in order to save money."

"Have you considered a short sale?"

"I did chat with a couple of real-estate agents. They tell me it's possible, but they say I'm upside down, which I'm told means my mortgage is greater than what I could sell the house for. By twenty to thirty thousand dollars. Coming up with January's payment will be hard enough. No way can I magically produce tens of thousands of dollars."

The lump in her throat moved down to lie heavy on her heart.

They chatted a few more minutes, and then Mr. Carter asked, "Have you considered renting the house out? We are in the middle of a local housing shortage."

"I have. But if I rent out my house, I'd need to find a place to live. I can't afford much on part-time wages." Not to mention she'd be giving up nursing.

"What about taking in boarders?"

"I looked into that, too." She thought she heard the sound of computer keys tapping in the background. "Not many people want to be roommates with a couple of senior citizens. And I can't take in someone with a pet or who has allergies because of my dog."

"Just for fun I pulled up some recent listings on the computer. I think you might be able to rent your house for close to what your monthly payment is."

"I can't see the average family wanting to rent a handicap-accessible house."

"No, but the county might. I just remembered they're looking for a house like yours."

"Whatever for?"

"A group home. Their rep contacted me a few weeks ago. I didn't think of you at the time."

"I'm not sure about that." Miranda imagined former convicts and drug addicts converging on Sweetheart. She couldn't do that to her neighbors. And it would be bad— really bad—for the town's tourist business.

"It's not what you think. This group home would be for special-needs teenagers the county's been unable to place in regular foster care."

Miranda's reluctance instantly evaporated. Her parents had taken in more than one special-needs child over the years. Letting Harmony House be used for such a meaningful and worthwhile purpose made renting it out a little more tolerable.

"Would you like me to make a call?" Mr. Carter asked.

"Yes. Ask them what they're willing to pay." Fact gathering, she told herself. She was in no way making a decision.

After saying goodbye, Miranda pulled out her laptop and powered it on. Once the wireless internet service connected, she clicked on the website for the hospital where she'd worked in Reno. Following the link for careers, she explored the current job openings.

More fact gathering, she reminded herself. As she'd told Will, leaving Sweetheart was her *very* last option.

She reviewed the available nursing positions with interest. There were four altogether. Two of them were a good fit with her experience and qualifications. One was for a geriatric nurse.

On impulse, she dialed the human resources department and, after identifying herself and her request, was put through to the supervisor of nursing. She remembered the woman from before. More important, the woman remembered Miranda. Favorably. They discussed the job openings, and Miranda, in too much of a rush to hunt down something to write on, scribbled notes on the side of a cardboard tissue box with an eyeliner pencil.

"When's the earliest you can come in for an interview?" the supervisor asked.

"Tomorrow." Miranda didn't care what appointments she had to shuffle. Christmas was in three days. If she didn't act quickly, she'd have to wait who knew how long. "Early afternoon would be best."

To her delight the woman replied, "Why don't I slot you in for one o'clock?"

"Perfect." Miranda could manage the round trip in less than three hours. Four if she stopped briefly to visit her parents. Nell would cover for her.

After a few parting pleasantries, Miranda ended the call. With trembling fingers, she phoned her parents. She'd need their help if she was going to return to Reno. Not for a loan but a bed to crash on until she found an apartment.

"Hey, Mom."

"Mira, what's wrong?"

Leave it to her mother to deduce Miranda had a problem by hearing two simple words.

Holding nothing back, she poured her heart out, telling her mother about losing her residents, her inability to refinance the mortgage, not wanting to leave Sweetheart because of Will and, lastly, her upcoming interview at the hospital.

"Am I making a mistake, Mom? These are big steps I'd be taking. I'd have to sign a two-year lease with the county on the house."

"Absolutely not. You're exploring your options."

"I don't want to lose Harmony House."

"You have nothing to be ashamed of, Miranda. What's happened to you is unexpected and unavoidable. A run of bad luck."

Until her mother said it, Miranda didn't realize how badly she'd needed confirmation that she hadn't screwed up. Wasn't a failure. Had done her best.

"There's no reason you can't reopen Harmony House in two years. God willing, the economy will be better by then."

Her house was only part of the problem. "I'm not sure about Will's reaction to a long-distance relationship. We're still in the beginning stages."

"Reno isn't that far. You can drive back and forth on your days off. Call. Text. Skype." Having raised numerous children, Miranda's mother was technologically savvy.

"It's not as simple as you think." Miranda sighed.

"It never is."

She explained Will's PTSD, omitting the personal details that were told to her in confidence. Being a nurse, too, her mother understood better than a layperson. She also understood the challenges of having a romantic relationship with someone who had the disorder.

"This is your mother talking," she said when Miranda finished. "While I'm sure Will is a great guy, he's obviously dealing with a lot right now. So are you. I don't think you should let your relationship with him factor into your decisions about the future of Harmony House and this potential nursing position. You have to look out for yourself."

What her mother said made sense. But Miranda's feelings for Will were too strong for her not to factor them into her decisions. How much they factored might well be up to him.

When Miranda hung up a short time later, she felt better about some things and worse about others. If only Will would accept the town's offer to be an EMT. That would put him in Reno two or three days a week. Once she found an apartment, he could stay with her. It was possible. His PTSD was improving.

She'd talk to him after the interview, she decided. And after Mr. Carter called about the house. No point doing it before then.

She'd no sooner turned off her laptop and headed for the stairs when her phone rang. It was Mr. Carter. Already?

"Glad I caught you," he said cheerily. "Just got off the phone with my contact from the county. They're still in the market for a property to rent. When I described your house and your situation, he was very interested."

Miranda made a dash for the tissue box and eyeliner pencil she'd left on the dresser and jotted down the man's number. "Thank you, Mr. Carter."

The man representing the county answered her call on the second ring. Before Miranda quite knew what was happening, she had an appointment with a property agent to tour the house the day after tomorrow. The morning before Christmas Eve.

It was all happening so fast.

Disconnecting her phone, she stared at herself in the dresser mirror, noting her drawn features and the anxious look in her eyes. Telling Will had just become a higher priority.

But not today and not with her looking the way she did. First she had the interview. Next she'd meet with the agent from the county.

Just because a plan of action had fallen into her lap was no reason to assume said plan was a done deal.

Except it seemed to Miranda that she was being guided in a direction. No longer a victim of fate's whims, she was taking charge. Being proactive.

If Will cared about her the way she believed he did, he'd see how much sense this plan made. She couldn't save her elder-care business, but she could keep her house *and* continue working as a nurse.

Two out of three wasn't bad, right?

"HAD ENOUGH FOR one day?" Will halted at the trailhead and punched one of his trekking poles deep into the snow for balance.

The grade in this spot was steep and his muscles were tired enough that he appreciated the extra support. His group of five fellow mountaineers had slowed their speed considerably during the past two hours, their five-mile jaunt on snowshoes wearing them out.

"No, no!" the young woman objected, the portion of her cheeks visible beneath her goggles a bright red. "Let's keep going."

"Are you crazy?" Her husband gaped at her, each word he spoke accompanied by a puff of white condensed air.

"Count me out." The other man's shoulders drooped beneath his parka. "I'm done in."

The woman was soundly outvoted. Will doubted she wanted to continue and was only showing off in front of the others. She'd been the most determined of the group from the start.

"This way." Will took the lead.

They crested the hill in single file, their steps hampered by the webbed snowshoes attached to their boots, and descended the other side. All of them were short of breath by the time they reached their vehicle.

Sam had recently purchased the all-wheel-drive SUV for a song, citing they needed one to transport guests into the mountains for cross-country skiing and, the ranch's newest offering, snowshoeing excursions.

Will had only recently taken up snowshoeing, but he liked it. Liked it better when he was alone and communing with the great outdoors in private. But this group had been good sports. In return he'd given them a hike to remember.

Lowering the SUV's tailgate, he instructed the beginners in the group on how to remove their gear. Had Miranda ever snowshoed? She was definitely the outdoors type, as she'd proved on their horseback ride. And having her for company wouldn't be bad at all. He'd have to ask her. Maybe after Christmas. After New Year's, he amended. She was overwhelmed these days.

Wait. After New Year's was when Mrs. Litey's brother would be moving her to Carson City. A snowshoe trek through the ice-cold mountains would be the last thing on Miranda's mind.

Will thought of her constantly. Though they'd talked by phone, he hadn't seen her since the day before yesterday. She'd pleaded a full schedule. He had a lot going on, too. The ranch was hosting an open house on Christmas Eve, Christmas Day dinner with sleigh rides afterward and a

New Year's Eve party. It was all hands on deck. Today's outing was Will's last one till the Monday after Christmas.

Unloading their backpacks and removing their gear took a while. Eventually the six of them were on the road back to town, the heater in the SUV set on high.

"Can we stop at the I Do Café?" The woman crossed her arms and hugged herself. "I could use a hot chocolate."

Her husband laughed. "I could use something a lot stronger."

A second show of hands was taken and, again, the woman was outvoted. Will dropped them off at the Paydirt Saloon. When they insisted he join them for a hot toddy, he declined with a promise to return in an hour. He had an errand to run that couldn't wait and drove straight to Dempsey's General Store and Trading Post.

"Hey, Will." Linda Lee, the store's assistant manager, beamed happily as he approached the counter. She wore a Santa hat with candy canes tucked in the brim. Will knew from when he'd stopped by the other day that she dispensed the candy canes to kids who came in the store. "They arrived," she informed him, a trill in her voice.

"Good." He'd worried the item he had ordered would be late. Deliveries were commonly detained in these parts, particularly after a storm.

"Be right back." She went through a door behind the counter to what Will assumed was a storeroom.

He'd debated for several days what to give Miranda for Christmas and even if he should give her anything at all. He wasn't expecting a gift in return. Money was tight for her, and he didn't want to embarrass her with a gesture she couldn't reciprocate.

In the end he decided to get her a gift. Then he'd been faced with the dilemma of what to buy her. The stores and boutiques in town were limited, most of them catering to the wedding trade. Driving to a larger metropolis was out of the question.

Linda Lee had come to his rescue. She'd also helped him pick out the gift and had tracked the package for him as it was shipped from Wyoming.

"She's going to love them." Linda Lee oohed and aahed as she opened the box for Will to inspect the contents. "Soft as a baby's behind."

Will removed the custom-designed leather gloves and held them in his hands. Not that he'd ever felt a baby's behind, but he thought Linda Lee might be right. Crackers had better not get hold of these. "Nice."

"Nice! They're divine. I'm so jealous. Miranda is one lucky lady."

Will was the lucky one, to have found a woman who could accept his PTSD and was willing to live with it. Even help him.

"Are you giving them to her at the open house?" Linda Lee propped her elbows on the glass counter and smiled dreamily. "Christmas Eve. Wouldn't that be romantic?"

When would he give Miranda the gloves? He hadn't thought that far ahead. Maybe on the way home from the Christmas Eve open house.

He missed her. Two days was too long to go without seeing her.

Several other customers had entered the store and were perusing the aisles. They assured Linda Lee they were simply browsing when she asked if they needed assistance.

"Thanks again, Linda Lee," he said. "For everything."

"You taking off?"

"I have a few minutes. Going to stop by Miranda's."

"She's not there." Linda Lee took the gloves from Will and carefully arranged them in the shipping box. She traced her finger over the distinctive logo before neatly enfolding the gloves in tissue paper.

"Hmm." If Will had known Miranda was working at the Paydirt, he'd have joined his group for their hot toddies.

"She went to Reno," Linda Lee continued. "The only reason I know that is because she stopped in here on her way out of town to use the copy machine."

"Reno?" Will frowned. Miranda hadn't mentioned leaving. "What's she doing there?"

"I haven't a clue. Must have had business. All I know is she wanted to use the special high-quality paper we have for her copies."

That was strange. What business did she have in Reno that she wouldn't tell him about? He instantly recalled their conversation in the sleigh the other day. She'd mentioned moving back to Reno as a possible solution to her financial troubles.

His stomach plummeted. She couldn't be considering a move. She'd told him no.

Linda Lee finished repacking the gloves, ignorant of the turmoil raging inside Will. With a flourish, she presented him with the box. "Good luck. You'll have to tell me how she likes them."

Muttering a distracted goodbye, Will left the store and jumped into the SUV, letting the engine warm a minute before taking off down the road toward Miranda's. He had thirty minutes before he needed to pick up his guests at the Paydirt.

Outside Harmony House, he parked alongside the curb and let the SUV idle. Miranda's van wasn't in the driveway but Nell's car was, and the dread he'd experienced earlier increased to an unbearable level. A panic attack hovered, waiting to strike.

He fought it. If there was ever a time Will needed to stay focused, this was it.

Taking out his cell phone, he dialed her number. The call went straight to voice mail. Leaving her a message, he tried to tell himself she was with her parents, accepting the loan they'd offered. Or at a meeting with another lending institution about refinancing her mortgage.

Any reason except investigating the possibilities of moving.

Will gripped the steering wheel with both hands and squeezed. Why hadn't she told him about her trip to Reno? His mind kept going back to that one important question.

Something was up. Something that didn't bode well for him.

For them.

Chapter Fourteen

"Hey, Will. How are you?" Miranda held the phone away from her ear and smiled apologetically at the property agent from the county. *I'll just be a second,* she mouthed.

No problem, the woman mouthed back. Removing a tape measure from her messenger bag, she indicated that she was going to check out the hall bathroom.

She'd already inspected the front room and kitchen, taking dozens of pictures with her camera and sticking her nose in every corner. All the holiday decorations didn't make her job any easier. Miranda half expected the woman to whip out a white glove and run her fingers along the tops of doors. Nell and her residents stood in the front room, their collective gazes following the agent's every move. Miranda shooed them away, but they didn't budge. She scowled at Nell, who gave an all-right-fine head bobble and shepherded the residents, plus Arthur, into the kitchen. She, however, remained, and no amount of glaring on Miranda's part got her to move from her spot.

Giving up, Miranda returned to the phone call from Will. "Sorry about that. How are you?"

"Good. I'm outside."

"What?" She started when a loud knock sounded from the front door. "You're here!"

"I just said that."

Oh, please, no! What had possessed him to show up

unannounced? Not returning his four phone messages be-tween yesterday and this morning, that was what.

She stalled. The last thing she wanted, needed, was for him to meet the property agent. "It really isn't a good time."

"Miranda, I'm standing at your door."

"Yes, um…" She couldn't very well leave him standing out there. But she couldn't let him in, either. Not until after the agent left. That left Miranda with only one option: con-vince Will to leave. "Hold on."

She ended their call and went to the door. Rather than letting him in, she stepped outside, closing the door behind her. Instantly cold air sliced through her thin sweater, and she wrapped her arms around her waist.

"Hi." She smiled while shifting from one foot to the other in an attempt to stay warm.

"What's going on?" he demanded.

"Nothing."

"Why won't you let me inside?"

She glanced guiltily behind her. "We're in the middle of packing. The place is a mess."

"As if I care."

He clearly wasn't going to leave without putting up a fight. "You're going to have to trust me. This isn't a good time."

"Why didn't you return my calls?"

"I should have, you're right. I had—have—a lot going on. I'll explain, I promise. Just give me an hour. Thirty minutes."

"Why did you go to Reno?"

She went still. "How did you find out?"

"Linda Lee told me."

Miranda could kick herself for blabbing, but she'd been so excited about the interview. Who'd have thought Will would have a conversation with the assistant manager at the general store?

"When did you run into her?"

"You're avoiding the question. And whose car is parked out front?"

"I'm cold." That was no lie. Her teeth had started to chatter. "Fine." She cut him off before he could pose another probing question. "You can come in. But, so help me, Will Dessaro, you keep your mouth shut, you hear? We'll talk later."

Of course, the county agent was right there in the front room when Miranda returned. Will stuck to her closer than a shadow. At the woman's raised eyebrows, Miranda made introductions.

"This is my friend, Will. He's a regular here. Visitor." Her laugh was forced. "Not a resident."

"Ah." The property agent smiled tightly, apparently not liking yet another interruption. "May I see the upstairs suite now?"

"Absolutely. Down the hall, first door on your left." Miranda didn't want to leave Will alone with the residents and Nell. It was a guaranteed fiasco.

"I have some questions," the woman said.

Her tone sent an unmistakable message. She hadn't liked being left on her own earlier when Miranda went outside to unsuccessfully detain Will.

Great, great, great. She was going to have to go upstairs with the woman and pray all went well.

"This way."

It was the longest ten minutes in Miranda's life. The property agent measured and counted everything, including how many electrical outlets there were and the dimension of the bathroom mirror. She noted the results in the portfolio she carried.

"Where does this vent lead?" she asked, running the toe of her shoe over a metal grill in the floor.

"It connects to the main vent running through the kitchen ceiling."

"And that leads to…?"

"The furnace over the garage."

She pursed her lips as she made another notation in the portfolio.

Was she thinking of possible escape routes? Miranda had spent several grueling months in a crowded youth facility before being placed with her foster parents. More than once she'd considered running away.

She couldn't believe the county would squelch the lease deal over a heating vent.

"I'm done here," the woman announced a few minutes later.

Hallelujah!

They descended the stairs. Miranda dreaded what awaited her. To her enormous relief, all was quiet. Maybe too quiet. She started for the kitchen, intending to check on her residents, but the property agent intercepted her.

Stowing her portfolio, tape measure and camera in her messenger bag, she said, "Thank you for your time, Ms. Staley. You have a very nice home."

"Does it suit the county's needs?" She wished she didn't sound so anxious.

"I'm not the one making that decision."

"But they rely on your recommendations."

The woman nodded, but said nothing to put Miranda's concerns at ease. "Someone will be in touch with you."

"How soon?" It wasn't like Miranda to be such a pest, but her entire financial future was riding on this.

The woman must have taken pity on her, because she paused at the front door and said, "In my opinion, your home is exactly what the county's looking for."

"That's wonderful!" Miranda pumped her fist enthusiastically.

She stood in the open doorway watching the woman walk to her car, no longer cold. With a sigh of relief, she turned—and came face-to-face with five expectant faces and a sixth stern one. Will's. With the exception of Babs in her wheelchair, they stood shoulder to shoulder.

"What's going on, Miranda?" Nell demanded, her thick arms shaking. "That wasn't any regular certification inspection."

"I'll explain." She shoved her fingers through her hair. This was not going as planned. "Just give me a minute."

"You're leasing the house."

Miranda's head shot up at Arthur's announcement and her eyes went wide. "What? How?"

"My granddaughter works part-time at the savings and loan. She overheard her boss talking."

Miranda was going to complain to Mr. Carter. The girl was out of line, spreading gossip about customers. Right after she thanked the loan officer for his help. If the county leased her house, and it looked as if they might, she'd be able to avoid foreclosure.

"Miranda?" Will's plea, even and low, cut straight through her.

Her throat closed and the strength went out of her legs. She collapsed onto the couch, abandoning all hope that this would go even the tiniest bit well.

"Tell us." Nell sat beside her on the couch and patted her leg. Everyone but Will crowded around her. "Are you losing the house?"

"A party." Mrs. Litey opened her arms wide to encompass the room. "How lovely. Let me get the hors d'oeuvres."

"It's all right, Mom." Will restrained her with a hand on her arm. "You don't have to do that."

She blinked in confusion. The next instant she was all smiles. "You're right. I should relax and enjoy myself. Let the caterers handle the food."

Miranda might have laughed if she wasn't on the verge of tears.

"About the house," Nell prompted.

"I'm trying my best *not* to lose it."

"By renting it out?"

"I can't afford the monthly payments on my wages from the Paydirt. And I can't operate Harmony House at a loss. The county's looking for a group home. The rent they'd pay me would cover my monthly mortgage."

"You're throwing us out?" Himey lamented.

She gentled her voice. "I told you two days ago. With Mrs. Litey leaving, I was probably going to close Harmony House. You and Babs need to find another place to live."

"We thought we had more time." Babs clutched at Arthur.

"Nothing's been finalized yet." Miranda turned to Nell. "I'm sorry. You've been the best employee. If I could—"

"Don't mind me," Nell assured her. "I'll find something. The Mountainside Motel is always hiring housekeepers."

They weren't. She was being optimistic.

"I'm more concerned about you, baby girl. What will you do?"

Miranda's glance went to Will. He'd been quiet up until now. Then again, he wasn't the talkative type. He didn't need to be. The man could say more with a quirk of his eyebrows than most people could with a hundred words.

"Miranda?" Nell repeated.

It hurt for Miranda to speak, but she had to answer. Maybe Will would respond better to her news in a crowd than if they were alone.

Yeah, who was she fooling?

"I've been offered a nursing job."

"At the clinic?" Nell clapped her hands together. "Praise the Lord."

"No, not at the clinic." Miranda focused on Will. "In Reno."

He closed his eyes, but not before Miranda witnessed the naked pain reflected in them. An invisible knife turned in her heart.

WILL HAD HAD no intention of following Miranda upstairs to her suite. He'd wanted to leave. Refused to stay there another second. Her announcement had shot a hole the size of a cannonball clear through him.

Then he'd felt the beginnings of a panic attack, invisible fists strangling him and cutting off his air supply. The door to her attic suite was closer than the front door, and there were less people blocking his path.

He stood in the center of her bedroom, snapping the rubber band on his wrist hard enough to leave small welts on his flesh.

She's been offered a job in Reno. That explained her mysterious trip and why she'd ignored his calls. Were there other secrets she was keeping from him?

Though the circumstances were different, he felt the same as when he and his former fiancée had split up. Her disappointment in Will, her inability to cope with his panic attacks, had caused her to leave him.

Was it the same with Miranda? He'd been so sure she was different.

Noises traveled up the stairs. Nell and the residents must be huddled together, deliberating the situation. They, like Will, had a lot to think about. A lot to discuss. Maybe, like him, they'd believed Miranda would never abandon them.

"Will, I'm sorry." She came over to where he stood.

He couldn't look at her and stared out the window. The bleak snow-covered landscape matched his insides.

She touched his arm, her caress soft. "Please talk to me."

When he said nothing, she threw herself at him, seeking his mouth with hers. So much for talking.

Any other time, he'd have kissed her senseless. Thrown her on the bed. Made sweet, incredible love to her. Not today. He was still too raw.

She abandoned her efforts a moment later, stepped back and covered her cheeks with her hands, her expression one of pure misery. "I guess Mom was wrong. A kiss doesn't make everything better."

"Why didn't you tell me about the job in Reno? Or leasing the house?"

She blew out a long breath. "I didn't see the sense in upsetting everyone until I knew for sure that the county was interested in the house, and I had a job lined up."

"We're all affected. Me, Nell and your residents." His anger grew. "You had no right to keep us in the dark."

"That wasn't my intention. Up until this morning, it was a long shot. Then the nursing supervisor called and the property agent showed up."

"But you hoped it would happen."

"Is that so wrong? I'm trying save my house and my credit rating." She groaned in frustration. "You think this is a decision I've made lightly?"

"Honestly, I'm not sure. From what I can tell, this just came up in the last couple days."

Her stance became defensive. "I can't operate Harmony House with only two residents. I'm barely scraping by with three and have to work twenty hours a week at the Paydirt to make up the difference."

That didn't change the fact that her unwillingness to confide in him hurt. "You should have told me."

"I would have. But the other day in the sleigh when I mentioned Reno, you kind of freaked out."

He had. Just as he did a few minutes earlier downstairs. He snapped the rubber band again.

"Don't make this my fault," he said.

"I had to take action, Will. I couldn't let my house go into foreclosure. This is a good solution."

"Why a job in Reno?"

"Why not Reno? I have family and friends there. The job is at the hospital where I used to work." She lowered her voice. "It won't be forever. The lease with the county is only for two years."

Two years? It sounded like a lifetime to him.

"Reno is only an hour away," Miranda continued to plead her case. "I'll come back on my days off."

How long until she grew tired of the drive? Tired of him?

"You could come to Reno."

All this time they'd spent together, everything she'd seen, and still she acted as if there was nothing wrong with him. "I can't."

"Will, listen to me." She placed herself in front of him. "Accept the town's offer. You can get the counseling you need to conquer your PTSD in Reno while you're training to be an EMT. I'll find a small apartment and you can stay with me. Between that and my trips here, we'll only be apart a few days a week."

The plan made sense for anyone but him.

"I don't start at the hospital till the first of February," she said. "Let's take a drive to Reno one day next week. Check out the EMT school. You can meet my family."

"I can't leave Sweetheart."

"Is it work? I'm sure Sam will give you a day off."

He looked straight at her. "I physically can't leave. I haven't for years."

"Of course you've left."

"No. Anytime I try, I get sick. Puke my guts out."

She drew back, frowning at him. "Why didn't you tell me?"

"Because I was afraid I'd lose you. Same as I lost Lexie."

"Oh, Will." She hugged him. He was slow to return it. "That wouldn't have happened."

But it was happening. He was losing her, too. History was repeating itself.

"When was the last time you tried leaving town?" she asked.

"Friday."

"And?"

"I made it an eighth of a mile out of town."

Understanding dawned on her face. "That's the real reason you didn't take the town's offer."

"Can't train to be an EMT if I can't get to the school."

"Don't give up. There are other techniques we haven't tried yet. Biofeedback. Meditation—"

"You're not listening to me," he snapped, pulling away from her.

"I am listening to you," she snapped right back at him. "And what I'm hearing is that you won't try."

"I have tried."

"Yes. Without the right kind of help and support. You need a professional therapist. You can't conquer this on your own."

She was turning the tables on him and he didn't like it. "My PTSD isn't the problem. You took a job in Reno without talking to me."

"I have no other choice." She sighed as if he, not her, was the one being single-minded.

"You do. You can stay here," he said. "Live with me."

"In your trailer?"

"It's not that bad."

"I'm no freeloader."

"Then keep working at the Paydirt."

"Nursing is too important to me to give up."

"It would only be temporary," he said, throwing her words back at her. "Or I can move in here with you." The idea had come from nowhere, but he wondered why he hadn't thought of it before. "We'll stay upstairs, and Babs and Himey can have the downstairs."

She went to the bed and sat on the edge. He thought she must have gone weak with relief. Such a simple solution, yet it would solve all her problems.

He joined her on the bed. "You can quit the Paydirt and take care of Babs and Himey full-time." At her look of alarm, he added, "Or keep working at the Paydirt if you don't want to let Nell go. I'm sure after the holidays you'll find a new resident."

"No."

"Why not? It's a great idea."

She shook her head. "I appreciate the offer, I know you're trying to help and have the sincerest of intentions. But I can't let you move in here just to save my house and business."

"That wouldn't be the only reason."

Did she not realize the extent of his feelings for her? Then again, had he ever told her how he really felt?

"If I wasn't on the brink of foreclosure, would you be asking to move in with me?" When he hesitated, she said, "I didn't think so."

"Lots of couples live together because it makes financial sense. You're being stubborn."

"Lots of couples don't..." She took a breath. "Don't have one partner with a debilitating condition."

He stiffened.

"Will, this isn't just about me or my house or my business." She cradled his cheek and forced his head toward her when he would have glanced away. "You won't get better if I continue accommodating you."

At least she hadn't used the term "enabling."

"I'm a lot better than I was."

"What you've done is improve your coping skills. And

avoided situations that trigger panic attacks. It's not the same thing as overcoming your condition."

"Sometimes coping is the best anyone with PTSD can do."

"I need more." Her voice was suddenly thick with emotion. "I need a man who will share my life completely. Who will go with me to visit my parents on their fortieth wedding anniversary or attend my brother's college graduation. A man who will take me on a fabulous honeymoon if we were to get married. Be by my side in the hospital if we were to have a child."

She gazed at him as if he meant the world to her. But if that were true, why wouldn't she stay in Sweetheart with him?

Unless she was using his PTSD as an excuse to break up with him. That was what his ex-fiancée had done.

"I can't leave. Won't leave."

"Not even for me?"

"Will you stay for *me?*"

She studied his face. "My situation is serious."

"Mine, too."

"Yours is treatable."

"And yours is fixable."

She withdrew, her features shutting down. "This isn't a contest to see which one of us has the bigger problem."

"Then quit making it into one."

Intended or not, his reply obviously hit the mark. She rose from the bed.

He did, too. "Miranda, wait. I don't think you comprehend the severity of my condition."

"Maybe I don't. But what I do comprehend is that you use it as a crutch. To avoid commitments."

That unnerved him. "I was ready to marry Lexie. Willing to leave the army for her."

"Really? Because I see a pattern here. You start getting close to someone, and *boom,* next thing you're having panic attacks."

Her aim was pretty good, too. "I could say the same about you."

"Me?"

"By your own admission, you haven't had a serious relationship in years."

"Because of work."

"It's always because of work. You're just as scared as I am. At least I'm willing to move in with you."

"On your terms. That we stay in Sweetheart and both of us, not just me, lose out on what could be a great opportunity."

"I thought Harmony House was your dream."

"It is. And I'll reopen it in a couple of years when the economy's improved and the town's recovered."

"In the meantime—"

"In the meantime, you and I can still have a relationship."

"Traveling back and forth between here and Reno?"

"Me working, saving money. You training to be an EMT and getting counseling."

"I can't," he reiterated, the memory of his last attempt at leaving still fresh in his mind.

She crossed her arms and glared at him. "You won't. Let's be clear on that."

He made one last attempt. "Stay, Miranda. We can't figure this out if you don't."

"I'm going to Reno. You might be content to live half a life, but I'm not." Her conviction left no doubt. She'd made her decision. "If you change your mind, you know where to find me."

There was no reason for Will to remain. Wordlessly he descended the stairs and left the house. He didn't turn around even when Mrs. Litey called his name. *His* name, not her son, Joseph's.

He drove straight to the ranch, feeling oddly calm. Cruze waited for him where he'd left him, guarding the horses in the corral. He stooped to give him a pat, which turned into a hug. He was where he belonged. At the Gold Nugget. With the horses and Cruze. Not with Miranda.

As he stroked the dog's thick fur, tolerated him licking his ear, something inside him snapped in two. Will could feel it, as if he was a giant tree split by lightning.

Miranda was leaving Sweetheart, going to Reno. He might not see her again for a long, long time.

Aware of guests milling about in the near distance, Will fled to the tack shed, making it in the nick of time. Leaning against a saddle rack, he stopped struggling…and suffered the worst panic attack of his life.

Chapter Fifteen

Christmas dinner at the Gold Nugget was a grueling affair for Will. Not because the food wasn't good or the company congenial. He'd spent a lousy two days after his blowup with Miranda.

He still couldn't believe she'd accepted a job in Reno and was leaving at the end of January. That she could so easily cast aside their relationship.

"Who wants dessert?" Sam's wife, Annie, carried one pie pan and one cake platter to the table. Her mother brought up the rear, balancing a large pot of coffee. "There's also some lime sorbet in the freezer."

The nine guests joining Sam's family at the table enthusiastically called out their preferences. Several complained that they didn't have room for another bite, only to accept the plate Annie waved in front of them.

"Will?" She smiled warmly at him. "What can I get you? Some of each?"

"Thanks, but no. I'm stuffed." He patted his stomach, which was on the empty side. He might have eaten more if each bite didn't taste like paste.

It was the same story last night at the ranch's open house. He'd made an appearance, for Sam's sake, stood in the corner for an hour, tossed back a whiskey, then left. If Sam had noticed, he didn't say. Then again, between his family and the guests, he was rather preoccupied.

"Come on," Annie coaxed. "I know how much you like desserts."

He did. That must be why Miranda was always offering him one. *Had* always offered him one. There would be no more trips to Harmony House. To see Mrs. Litey or for any other reason.

"If you don't mind, I'm going to excuse myself." Will crawled out of the bench seat, narrowly avoiding kicking his neighbors. "Sorry," he murmured.

"What about the sleigh ride?" one of the guests asked.

Damn. He'd forgotten.

"Heading to the barn now to hitch up." Only when he was outside did he realize he'd run off without his coat.

There was an old one hanging in the barn. He headed there first to collect Cruze and the draft mare. To his relief he discovered a pair of gloves in one of the coat pockets.

Leading Sugar Pie to the tack shed, he tied her to the hitching post in front and looked around. He hadn't been back since his last panic attack. Then, the shed had seemed to shrink until the walls had completely closed in on him. Today it was normal size. And yet he still felt as if he couldn't draw a decent breath.

Reaching under the cuff of his shirtsleeve, he began snapping the rubber band on his wrist and silently chanting his mantra. Both coping mechanisms failed completely. No surprise.

Will wasn't having a panic attack. He was suffering from a broken heart.

He loved Miranda. Had since the day of the fire evacuation when she'd come scurrying down the attic stairs. Perhaps even from his first day in Sweetheart when he'd bumped into her at the general store.

Why hadn't he told her? It might have made a difference. Caused her to choose staying over leaving.

Wishful thinking on his part. What was it she'd said?

She wanted a man who could go with her to her parents' anniversary party. Take her on a honeymoon. Be by her side during the birth of their child.

Would Will be able to leave Sweetheart for something as important as that? Important as any of those things were?

Miranda wasn't being unreasonable. She wanted an emotionally and mentally healthy partner. So had Will's ex-fiancée. The difference was Miranda had claimed to want to help him through the healing process. In the end both women had run for the hills.

Will began removing the harness from where it hung on the rack, and then laid it out. First the collar, then the bridle. Last the long reins, which required a bit of straightening. Cruze lay with one front paw crossed over the other, watching patiently.

Will heard a telltale creak but didn't look up from his task, even when Cruze's tail thumped on the hard floor.

"You intend to hide out all Christmas Day in here?" Sam stood in the doorway.

"Only if I can convince you to drive the sleigh."

Sam stepped inside. "Not a chance. I promised Annie I'd spend the afternoon with her and the girls."

"Then I guess I'm done hiding out."

"At least you admit it."

"I've been admitting a lot of things to myself the last few minutes."

"Usually works better when you tell others." Sam's eyes were kind, not judgmental. "I take it you and Miranda had a disagreement."

"More like a parting of ways."

Sam stepped closer. "I'm sorry, buddy."

"Me, too." Will felt the hurt anew, a giant lead weight filling his chest. "She's leaving Sweetheart. Accepted a nursing job in Reno."

"What about Harmony House?"

"She's renting it out to the county. For two years." Will explained the lease agreement. "It was that or foreclose on her mortgage."

"I'm not trying to be insensitive," Sam said, "but I don't see the issue here. Go to Reno with her. I'll find another trail boss. Better yet, accept the town's offer for EMT training."

Was everyone talking about him behind his back? Miranda had uttered almost those exact same words.

"I can't leave. You know that."

"You won't leave, you mean."

Again, the same words. Were they in cahoots? Will was starting to feel ganged up on. He opened his mouth only to shut it. Miranda and Sam were both right. Will had just realized as much himself ten minutes ago.

"It's not as easy as you think," he said after a pause.

"I don't think it's easy at all. But if it came down to me losing Annie or doing something difficult, nearly impossible, I'd choose Annie always. Love's funny that way. It makes you into Superman. Faster than a speeding bullet. More powerful than a locomotive. Able to leave Sweetheart and go to Reno."

Will ground the heel of his palm into his forehead. He wanted to believe Sam. "I don't know if I can."

"I'll go with you."

"No." Too humiliating if he failed. "I have to do this myself."

"See." Sam cracked a grin. "You're already talking like Superman."

Will took stock of himself. Damned if he wasn't feeling stronger. "Okay, I'll do it. Tomorrow."

"Today."

"The guests are expecting a sleigh ride."

"They'll wait."

"This may take a while."

"Then I'll drive the sleigh."

"What about Annie and the girls?"

"Quit coming up with excuses and get out of here."

Who was Will to disobey an order from his boss?

Whistling for Cruze, he hurried to his truck. He might need the calming effects of his canine pal if he hoped to accomplish the impossible. Cruze leaped onto the passenger seat when Will opened the door. The engine protested the cold weather, blowing out thick white streams of exhaust.

Once the truck was warmed, Will drove to the edge of town. He made it a full quarter mile before nausea overtook him. He stopped by the road and gave himself a few minutes to rest, during which he thought of Miranda constantly.

It did the trick. When his stomach settled, he drove another full quarter mile. Not bad. A whole lot better than before, in fact. At the first mile marker out of town, he was forced to stop again. Picturing Miranda's face got him back on the road.

Son of a bitch! He could do this. Sam was right!

Instead of continuing, Will turned the truck around and drove back to town, straight to Miranda's house. He had to tell her.

At her front door, he ground to a halt, his fist raised in the air. Tell her what, exactly?

I love you. I support you. I will go with you to Reno. Anywhere you want. I'm sorry I was such a jerk.

His fist came down hard on the door.

"Well, Merry Christmas to you, too," Nell said when she answered his frantic knocking.

"Where's Miranda?" Will started to squeeze past the plump woman.

"Not here."

The floor seemed to buckle beneath his feet. "Where is she?"

"Reno, you silly. Visiting her family. She left yesterday."

"She was supposed to have dinner here with the residents." He must have chased her away. "When will she be back?"

"Tomorrow. Late morning. She has an appointment with the county. To sign that lease and finalize some other paperwork."

He was too late.

Nell grabbed his arm. "Get yourself inside. You look as if you're ready to collapse. Sit down and I'll fetch you some water."

Will let her drag him along like a child and deposit him on the couch.

"She was crying when she left," Arthur said.

"What?" Will's head snapped up. He'd thought he was alone.

"The poor girl hates closing Harmony House and moving." The elderly gentleman, as always, sat in a chair beside Babs, holding her hand. She looked on the verge of tears herself.

"She's not the only one."

"What are you going to do about it?" Arthur asked.

"Stand by her."

"We were hoping you'd stop her."

"I offered to move in here. She turned me down."

"Did you make the offer on bended knee?"

"Uh…no."

Arthur harrumphed. "Youngsters. They have no clue."

Before Will could explain himself, Nell returned with the water. He drained the glass. It steadied his nerves.

"How's Mrs. Litey?"

The caregiver shook her head. "Miserable. She doesn't want to leave, either. Himey's been in his room all day, moping. This has been the worst Christmas ever." She glanced at Arthur and Babs, a smile spreading across her face. "Well, not the worst."

Arthur ginned like a schoolboy and kissed the back of Babs's hand. "We're getting married."

Will blinked. "You are?"

"My daughter and son-in-law agreed to let Babs live with us. I told them I wouldn't dream of it without making an honest woman of her first." He kissed Babs's hand again. "She's accepted and made me the happiest man alive."

"Congratulations," Will stammered. He wasn't much of a romantic, but there was something incredibly touching about the older couple.

Nell sniffed. "You better invite me to the wedding."

"Of course!" Babs glowed. "Everyone at Harmony House is invited."

"It's going to be hard on my family," Arthur conceded. "They don't have much room in their house. And, let's be honest, one crotchety old person is one crotchety old person too many." He gazed lovingly at Babs. "Not that you have a crotchety bone in your body, my dear."

"Oh, Arthur." She planted an affectionate kiss on his mouth.

"It's too bad things aren't different," he said. "If Mrs. Litey wasn't leaving, I'd move in here with Babs. Then there'd be four of us for Nell to boss around and no reason for Miranda to lease the house."

"I'm not bossy." Nell's eyes twinkled even as she voiced a loud protest.

Will kept hearing what Arthur had said.

If Mrs. Litey wasn't leaving, I'd move in here with Babs.
If Mrs. Litey wasn't leaving.

He stood and started down the hall.

"Where are you going?" Nell hollered.

"Be right back."

As usual, Mrs. Litey was sitting in her chair. She glanced up in surprise as he entered her bedroom.

"Merry Christmas, Mrs. Litey."

"How nice to see you, Will."

Will. Not Joseph. He almost missed her thinking he was her son. In a way he'd lost his grandmother all over again.

Taking the empty chair adjacent to hers, he said, "I have a favor to ask you."

"What's that?"

Not all Mrs. Litey's days were good ones. Lucky for Will, today was. "I need your brother's address."

"Why?"

"Do you want to move to Carson City with him?"

"Heavens, no! I love Sweetheart. It's my home. I grew up here. Married my husband in the Yeungs' wedding chapel. Buried him in the Hilltop Cemetery." Her eyes grew moist. "What if I never get to visit him again?"

"I think I can help you. Help all of us."

"How?" Her voice warbled.

"By visiting your brother."

Once he finished telling her of his plan, she gave him her brother's address without hesitation, looking it up in the small notebook she kept. Fifteen minutes later, Will was once more in his truck, Cruze beside him in the passenger seat. They took the south road out of town.

He'd traveled no more than a mile when he was hit with a debilitating wave of nausea. He kept driving, however, fighting off the sickness. Too much was riding on this: Harmony House, the residents' future, Nell's, too. And most important, the life he and Miranda could have together.

"REVEREND DONAHUE?" WILL asked, removing his cowboy hat.

"Have we met?" The distinguished older gentleman stood in his doorway, his smile friendly but his manner slightly guarded.

Will understood. He'd be wary if a stranger showed up

at his door late afternoon on Christmas Day. Especially one who looked how Will did.

A quick check in his rearview mirror had almost caused him to throw the truck in Reverse. His hair was disheveled, the result of him constantly shoving his fingers into it. His shirt was rumpled, having been soaked with sweat, which dried and soaked again. His eyes were those of a wild man.

But Will had made it to Carson City. In one piece, as far as he could tell. He hadn't died. Hadn't wanted to. Several times en route, he'd been forced to stop and wait until he was able to resume driving. Thoughts and images of Miranda had given him the strength and determination to push through and keep going. The pep talk from Sam was his mantra.

"No, sir," Will said. "But I've heard a lot about you. I'm well acquainted with your sister."

"Which one? I have three."

That threw him for a loop. "Um…Mrs. Litey."

"Leonora?" Interest flickered in the reverend's eyes, but he didn't invite Will inside, despite the cold. "How are you two acquainted?"

"My name's Will Dessaro. I live in Sweetheart and met your sister last summer when I helped Miranda, I mean Ms. Staley, evacuate the residents. Mrs. Litey, Leonora, she believes I'm Joseph. Did believe I was him. She's much better now."

"You're that young man! I've heard so much about you." He gestured Will inside, his stilted movements and gnarled hands indicative of advanced arthritis. "You look as if you have something heavy weighing on your mind."

"You're good at reading people."

"Comes with the job."

Delicious smells assailed Will the moment he crossed the threshold. "I've interrupted your dinner."

"Not at all. Some of my former parishioners stopped by

and brought me leftovers. Much more than I can eat alone. Have you had your dinner?"

"I don't want to impose."

"Join me, please. Conversation always flows easier over good food. You can tell me what brought you all this way to see me."

Will had expended a lot of energy, physical and emotional, getting to Carson City, and he was starved.

"Thank you."

Reverend Donahue prepared two plates of turkey, stuffing, green beans, sweet potato casserole and cranberry sauce. He topped the meal off with homemade rolls.

Will had consumed half his meal before he stopped long enough to breathe. "Sorry," he murmured, embarrassed.

"Nothing wrong with a healthy appetite." The reverend put down his fork. "Tell me about Ms. Staley."

"It's your sister I want to talk to you about."

"You didn't drive fifty miles on Christmas Day and in this weather to talk about my sister."

Will swallowed the bite of turkey and dressing he'd been chewing. "I did, sir. Both of them, actually."

Reverend Donahue listened intently as Will explained Miranda's situation and the fate of Harmony House. Also how he'd come to know Mrs. Litey and spend time with her.

"You must be very fond of her," the reverend said when Will had finished.

"Of both of them."

"They're lucky to have you championing them."

Nice but not what Will wanted to hear. "If you remove your sister from Harmony House and the town she's lived in her entire life, she may regress."

"You're right. There's a risk." The reverend's tone was thoughtful. "But I promised myself when I retired from the pulpit, I'd dedicate myself to taking care of Leonora. This house is more than big enough, and my days are filled with too many empty hours."

"Excuse me for saying this, Reverend, but it sounds as if you'd be moving Mrs. Litey because it's best for you and not for her."

"You're certainly direct. I respect that in a person." He leaned back in his chair. "As children, Leonora and I were thick as thieves. As adults, I'm sorry to say, we grew apart. My work and life were here, hers were in Sweetheart. It's no wonder she doesn't recognize me when I call. I'm going to change that."

"And if she gets worse?"

"There are places she and I can get help. More in Carson City than in Sweetheart."

"If she stays in Sweetheart, she may not need that help."

"Young man—"

"Miranda is losing her elder-care business."

The reverend became pensive. "I am sorry about that."

"Come with me to Sweetheart," Will said impulsively. "Today. Visit your sister before you make a final decision."

"It's kind of late for that."

"You can stay at the Gold Nugget. I'll bring you back tomorrow."

"I don't know…"

"Please, sir."

Reverend Donahue shook his head. "You love Miranda, and it's natural that you'd fight for her. But there's more at stake here."

Will didn't correct the man. He was in love with Miranda *and* he was fighting for her. Nothing would stop him until he'd given it his all.

"I'm not just thinking of Miranda. Two more residents of Harmony House are being forced out with nowhere to go." Okay, that was an exaggeration. Babs had Arthur. Himey's fate, however, was uncertain. "There's also her caregiver, Nell, who's losing her job."

"Have you ever considered a career in used car sales?" The reverend smiled. "You'd be good at it."

"Come home with me. See your sister. Miranda's been good to her and deserves this one last chance. Who knows, you might like it there and decide to live in Sweetheart." Will's off-the-wall remark earned him a hearty laugh.

"I can't just move on a whim."

"Why not? You're retired."

"A situation I'm not happy about. These joints of mine have slowed me down." He rubbed his hands together. "If not for that, I'd still be preaching on Sunday mornings."

"Sweetheart doesn't have a minister."

"I find that hard to believe."

"We had three before the fire. And a justice of the peace. They all left. Now the only official in town able to marry people is the mayor."

"Has the wedding business picked up again?"

"It's starting to. The mayor and town council are planning a Mega Weekend of Weddings that, they say, will put us back on the map. We could use a new minister."

He shook his head. "There's still my sister."

"Let her stay at Harmony House. She's happy there. You could visit her every day. Take her on outings. The residents toured the Gold Nugget recently. Mrs. Litey came alive."

"I bet she did. She always loved that ranch."

He was softening, Will could sense it. He made one last pitch, agreeing he might have missed his calling as a used car salesman.

"If you still want to move her after your visit, I'll help you. She won't cooperate, and you'll need me."

He crooked a bushy silver brow at Will. "You'd do that? Even though it's not what you want?"

"I have faith."

The reverend smiled. "A man in my profession likes hearing that." He stood and gathered their plates. "Help me clean the kitchen. I can't very well leave with a sinkful of dirty dishes."

Will jumped from his chair, grinning foolishly. "Do you like dogs?" He reached for their empty glasses.

"Love them. Why do you ask?"

"You'll be sharing your seat during the drive."

"Well, in that case, I'd better be prepared." The reverend placed a few turkey scraps in a plastic bag.

Will decided this just might be a merry Christmas after all.

Chapter Sixteen

"Miranda. Miranda! Where in blue blazes are you?" Nell burst into the storeroom off the garage, her face flushed from exertion. "Thank God I found you."

Miranda sprang to her feet, scattering the items she'd been organizing for future packing. "What's wrong?" She hurried toward Nell, visions of Mrs. Litey falling in the tub or Himey having a heart attack.

"We have visitors." Nell took hold of the nearest shelf, breathing as if she'd run a marathon.

"Visitors? Is that all?" Miranda stooped to pick up a toppled plastic basket. "Good grief, you gave me the scare of my life. Who's here?"

Some neighbors had probably stopped by for a little day-after-Christmas holiday cheer. Miranda could use some cheer, though she wasn't in the mood to see people.

Signing the lease with the county been difficult. So difficult, in fact, that she hadn't done it. Instead she'd asked for more time to review the documents, saying she wanted her lawyer to look at them. Miranda had left Reno that morning sad and miserable, knowing what she should do but dreading it.

Packing was supposed to keep her from obsessing about leaving her home, closing her business and losing Will. It hadn't worked. The only bright spot in her day had been learning about Babs and Arthur's engagement.

"You've got to come now," Nell insisted, finally recovering. And was that an excited grin she wore?

"What's going on?"

"Will's here." Apparently at her wit's end, Nell grabbed Miranda by the arm and physically removed her from the storeroom.

"Will?" Miranda was just coming to terms with that bit of news when Nell dropped a second bombshell.

"He brought Mrs. Litey's brother with him."

"Reverend Donahue?"

"Isn't that what I just told you?" Nell rolled her eyes. "Honestly."

Both women stumbled through the garage and into the kitchen.

"When did the reverend arrive in town?" Miranda asked.

"Last night. Will brought him. He stayed at the Gold Nugget. They've been waiting for you to come home."

"The reverend lives in Carson City."

"That's right. Will went there and got him."

Miranda ground to a halt. "Impossible. He can't leave Sweetheart."

"I reckon he can, if it's important enough. You must be pretty important to him."

Nell couldn't be more wrong. If Miranda really was important to Will, he wouldn't have walked out on her the other day. Nell must also be wrong about him driving to Carson City.

At the sink, Miranda hastily washed the grime from her hands, then finger combed her messy hair. Why hadn't she put on makeup today?

What difference did it make? Will wasn't there to see her; he'd accompanied Mrs. Litey's brother. Besides, they weren't dating anymore. She shouldn't care about how she looked, and she didn't.

Miranda glimpsed herself in the small mirror on the

wall beside the refrigerator and quickly wiped a smudge from her cheek.

"You look fine," Nell admonished with will-you-hurry-up impatience.

Miranda slowly entered the front room. Will stood there, the reverend at his side, Crackers dancing in circles in a bid for attention.

The two halves of her broken heart beat for the first time in three days.

"Merry Christmas, Miranda. It's a pleasure to see you again. Been too long." Reverend Donahue stepped forward, his hand extended. "I hope you'll pardon our interruption."

"I— It's fine. You're welcome...anytime." Her mouth didn't move as fast as her brain, which was racing.

"I want to see Leonora one last time before making a final decision about moving her. Will here insisted. Drove all the way to Carson City to convince me."

"He did?" Her gaze traveled to Will. "To Carson City?"

He nodded.

"How?"

He didn't take his eyes off her. "One mile at a time."

A nondescriptive answer that revealed nothing. And everything.

Nell was right. Miranda *was* important to Will. The gaping rift inside her began to mend.

"Any chance I can see my sister?" the reverend asked.

"Absolutely!" Miranda started toward the hall, continually glancing backward at Will.

He lingered until the reverend called for Will to join them. He and Miranda waited outside Mrs. Litey's room while the reverend went in.

Miranda was acutely aware of Will's proximity. Of the heat his body generated. Of his eyes never leaving her face.

He'd driven all the way to Carson City to bring back

Mrs. Litey's brother. She was still trying to grasp the full meaning of that.

"Why?" she whispered to him.

His reply was to take her hand in his and hold it tight.

That was all the answer she needed.

"Leonora?" The reverend approached the bed and spoke softly.

Mrs. Litey sat up, pillows bolstering her back, staring out the window. At the sound of her name, she turned to face her brother and glared.

This was not one of her good days.

"Who are you?" she demanded.

The reverend looked crushed.

Tears stung Miranda's eyes. She wished she could wave a magic wand and make Mrs. Litey remember her brother.

Suddenly Mrs. Litey pushed the blankets aside. "Corky?" She struggled to fasten the belt to her robe. "Corky, for the love of Pete, what are you doing here?"

Corky?

"Leonora." The reverend, visibly moved, collected Mrs. Litey in his arms as she rose unsteadily from the bed. "I'm here, sis."

"Who's Corky?" Miranda asked.

"Reverend Donahue. That's her nickname for him," Will said. "He told me on the drive here."

"Mrs. Litey must think they're still children."

"No, she doesn't." Will nodded at the pair.

The two senior siblings were hugging and laughing. It was a reunion many years overdue.

"I'm so glad for them." Miranda's emotions threatened to overwhelm her.

"We should probably give them some time alone."

Miranda agreed. She and Will went out into the front room where, in their absence, Arthur had arrived. As usual, he hovered by Babs's side. Himey had emerged from his room for the first time that morning.

Miranda sighed. She would miss them all terribly.

Nell, God love her, had prepared rounds of nonalcoholic eggnog, and the group toasted Babs and Arthur's engagement. Miranda wanted to get Will alone and ask him about his trip, and what, if anything, his newfound ability to leave Sweetheart meant for them and their future.

A few minutes later, Mrs. Litey and the reverend joined them. Miranda's questions for Will were put on hold while another toast was made to honor the siblings.

"I can't thank you enough." Reverend Donahue approached Will and shook his hand. "You've given me back my sister." He looked to Miranda. "You, too. She's almost her old self."

"I'm so glad."

"I realize it may not last."

She smiled sympathetically. "Unfortunately, people with Alzheimer's don't generally make spontaneous or lasting recoveries. But they can improve."

"Which seems to be the case here."

Mrs. Litey came over to stand beside her brother and linked her arm through his. "Did you tell them?"

"I was just about to. I've decided—Leonora and I *together* have decided—that she's going to remain here. In Harmony House."

"Oh, Reverend." Miranda was deeply moved. "I can't tell you how much that means to me, that you'd let her stay."

"Do I hear a but coming?"

"As much as I want to…" Her gaze encompassed all the people so dear to her. "The plain fact is I'm not making enough money to keep Harmony House open. This last month I've had to work part-time at the Paydirt Saloon in order to make ends meet. I was hoping to start an adult day-care program after the holidays." She paused. "But that isn't going to happen, either."

"Miranda," Mrs. Litey said with obvious concern, "you can't close down Harmony House."

It was the first time in months Mrs. Litey had addressed Miranda by her name. She wished it had been under better circumstances.

"I have no choice. Things might have been different if I'd been able to refinance my mortgage. But the savings and loan turned me down. Twice."

"Have you tried another lending institution?" the reverend asked.

"They'd have the same requirements as my current one. Namely that I bring in more income than my expenses."

"I might be able to help."

Miranda couldn't stop herself and chuckled. "You're in the mortgage business, too?"

"No." He laughed in return. "My business is, was, serving my congregation. One of the benefits, however, is getting to know people from all walks of life. Including banking."

Miranda narrowed her gaze. "Are you saying you have connections?"

"I am. If you wish, I could make a few phone calls on your behalf. There's a favor or two owed to me I can collect on. Land you a meeting, at least."

"That would be truly wonderful, Reverend."

He looked at her questioningly. "I'm hearing another but."

She sighed. "Even with a lower mortgage payment, and that's if I'd qualify, two residents just isn't enough. Babs is leaving to marry Arthur and live with his family. I need to stick to my plan and take the nursing job in Reno."

"What if you had four residents? Not two." Everyone turned to look at Arthur. "I could move in here. If you'd give Babs and me the big bedroom."

"Your daughter—"

"The heck with her." He winked at Babs. "I'd sure as shootin' rather live here with my beautiful new wife than in my daughter's home. Babs would, too."

"Arthur, I love you." Babs's eyes grew teary.

"Are you serious?" Miranda had to be sure.

"Never been more serious in my life," Arthur said.

"It's settled, then," the reverend boomed, and gave Miranda a bear hug. "You're keeping Harmony House."

She was?

She *was*. "I am!"

Miranda was instantly surrounded. Hugs and kisses on the cheek were freely dispensed. Will's was the most meaningful.

"Thank you," she told him, love filling all the previously empty places in her. "Money will still be tight, but now at least I can hang on until I find a fifth resident."

"What if that fifth resident didn't need elder care?"

"I thought about taking in boarders. Not sure that would work. And I might lose my certification."

"Not a boarder. A husband."

A thrill coursed through her, illuminating her from the inside out. "What are saying?"

"This wasn't how I planned it." His hands shook and his breathing became shallow.

She reached for him. "Are you all right?"

"I'm fine, I think." He struggled for air.

"Here." She took his arm. "You need to sit down."

"I don't."

"You're having a panic attack."

"I'm not." He swallowed. "I'm just nervous."

"About what?"

"Proposing. To you."

"Eeek!" The loud squeal came from Nell.

Miranda was shocked into silence for, perhaps, the first time in her life.

"Don't say yes yet," Will told her. "I need help. Lots of it. With my PTSD. I can get it, too, while I'm in Reno. Going to school."

She found her voice. "You're accepting the town's offer!" That made her almost as happy as his proposal.

"Yeah. Now that I know I can make the drive. I have you to thank for that."

"You did it on your own."

"I love you, Miranda. I'm only sorry it took me five years to work up the courage to tell you."

"I love you, too." She launched herself at him, hugging him fiercely.

"Is that a yes?"

She buried her face in his shirt. "Only if you're sure. There are a lot of people living in this house. You won't feel…crowded?"

"I think it's long past time I felt crowded." He kissed her then, in front of everyone and with no reservation or shyness.

She definitely liked this brand-new Will.

"I told you so," Nell declared when they broke apart.

"Well, well," the reverend said. "Appears I have my first two weddings to perform. That is, if you want me to officiate."

"When's the soonest you're available?" Arthur asked. "My darling and I are in a hurry."

"Pick a date."

"Should we wait until the Mega Weekend of Weddings?" Babs asked.

"That's not till this summer." Arthur went down on one knee in front of her wheelchair and took her delicate hands in his. "I can't wait that long. I can hardly wait till this weekend. Marry me next Saturday."

"You are truly the man of my dreams." She cradled his face and pressed her lips to his.

Miranda didn't think she'd ever seen anything sweeter.

Until a while later when Will whisked her upstairs to her room after all the commotion had died down. There he, too, went down on bended knee in front of her as she sat on the bed.

"I want no other woman than you, Miranda, and never will. I will do my dead level best to make you happy."

"You already have." She pulled him onto the bed with her, accepting his proposal for the second time. How could she not? He'd done the impossible for her: driven to Carson City and brought back the reverend. Saved her home and her business. Made her life complete.

"I feel bad about telling the county no," Miranda said as they lay spooned together. Just holding and touching.

"Who's to say you can't open a second Harmony House? One for foster teenagers."

She sat up. "You think I could?"

"I think you can do anything. Talk to the county. Have Sam's construction contractor remodel one of the abandoned houses in town."

"Will, that's an incredible idea."

"Then the contractor can build us a new house."

"Us?"

"I need a place to park the town's fire truck. And I'm not living in your attic forever. Especially after we start having a bunch of kids."

"You want a family?"

"I do. With you. And I don't care if they're biological or fosters."

"What about one of each?" she asked.

"Just one?"

She was too busy covering his face with kisses to give him an answer.

Epilogue

Will stood at the altar, waiting for the bride to make her entrance. His palms were clammy and sweat soaked the collar of his tuxedo shirt, making his neck itch like crazy. He tried not to fidget; this was no time for a panic attack, but Arthur noticed.

"You got ants in your pants, young man?"

"No, sir," Will whispered.

"Steady, gents," Reverend Donahue warned, a serene grin on his face, the Bible in his hands open to the page he would read during the wedding ceremony.

"I'm fine," Will said, and he was.

This New Year's Day was one of celebration. His and Miranda's lives lay stretched before them, full of endless possibilities and unlimited potential.

Suddenly the rear door to the chapel opened, and the strains of "Here Comes the Bride" filled the room. The entire assembly stood as the bride and her escort appeared. There were very few dry eyes in the sanctuary. The people gathered weren't just watching any wedding. This couple was two of their own, and that made the occasion special.

Will couldn't take his eyes off Miranda as she walked slowly down the aisle pushing Babs's wheelchair. She'd been honored when the elderly woman had requested Miranda give her away. Will had been equally honored when Arthur had asked him to serve as best man.

He tried to pay attention during the ceremony. It was hard. Miranda completely captivated him. He stared more at the pew where she sat after giving Babs away than at the wedding couple. It took two reminders from Reverend

Donahue and one poke in the ribs from Arthur to pull Will out of his trance. With a sheepish grin, he handed Arthur the simple gold ring from his pocket.

Nell, who was Babs's matron of honor, shook her head. "*Men.* I swear."

At the reverend's words, "I now pronounce you husband and wife," everyone cheered and applauded. When he said, "You may now kiss your bride," Will went over to Miranda, hauled her out of the pew and claimed her mouth with a warm kiss. More cheers followed.

It was Arthur who pushed Babs back down the aisle during the lively wedding march. Will took Nell's arm, doing as he'd been instructed and walking her down the aisle after the newly married couple.

She swatted him away. "Good gracious, leave me be. Miranda's the one you want to be pawing."

He did. Escorted Miranda from the sanctuary, that is. At the end of the aisle, he bent to whisper in her ear. "Next time we're in this chapel will be for our wedding."

Outside in the atrium, the wedding party assembled in a line to receive the guests. Will and Miranda were noticeably absent. They'd snuck off to the bride's dressing room.

Will had learned to tolerate large crowds. He even liked them. But there were moments when nothing beat privacy. He took full advantage of this one—and would again, every chance he got, for the rest of his and Miranda's lives together.

* * * * *

Watch for the next book in Cathy McDavid's
SWEETHEART, NEVADA *trilogy,*
MOST ELIGIBLE SHERIFF,
coming March 2014
only from Harlequin American Romance!

COMING NEXT MONTH FROM

HARLEQUIN

American Romance

Available December 3, 2013

#1477 THE TEXAS CHRISTMAS GIFT
McCabe Homecoming • by Cathy Gillen Thacker
Eve Loughlin is completely unsentimental about Christmas.
That is, until she falls for Derek McCabe and his infant daughter,
Tiffany, who have Christmas in their hearts all year long!

#1478 THE COWBOY'S CHRISTMAS SURPRISE
Forever, Texas • by Marie Ferrarella
Cowboy Ray Rodriguez has been looking for love in all the
wrong places. He never suspected after one night with a
longtime friend, the sweet and loyal Holly, he'd be tempted
with forever.

#1479 SECOND CHANCE CHRISTMAS
The Colorado Cades • by Tanya Michaels
Bad boy Justin Cade has no interest in starting a family. Yet,
thanks to Elisabeth Donnelly, his ex, and the six-year-old
girl she's adopted, Justin finds himself visiting Santa Claus,
decorating Christmas trees...and falling in love.

#1480 THE SEAL'S CHRISTMAS TWINS
Operation: Family • by Laura Marie Altom
Navy SEAL Mason Brown gets the shock of his life when his
ex-wife leaves him custody of her twin daughters in her will.
He's a soldier—not daddy material!

YOU CAN FIND MORE INFORMATION ON UPCOMING HARLEQUIN® TITLES,
FREE EXCERPTS AND MORE AT WWW.HARLEQUIN.COM.

HARCNM1113

REQUEST YOUR FREE BOOKS!
2 FREE NOVELS PLUS 2 FREE GIFTS!

HARLEQUIN

American ★ *Romance*®

LOVE, HOME & HAPPINESS

YES! Please send me 2 FREE Harlequin® American Romance® novels and my 2 FREE gifts (gifts are worth about $10). After receiving them, if I don't wish to receive any more books, I can return the shipping statement marked "cancel." If I don't cancel, I will receive 4 brand-new novels every month and be billed just $4.74 per book in the U.S. or $5.24 per book in Canada. That's a savings of at least 14% off the cover price! It's quite a bargain! Shipping and handling is just 50¢ per book in the U.S. and 75¢ per book in Canada.* I understand that accepting the 2 free books and gifts places me under no obligation to buy anything. I can always return a shipment and cancel at any time. Even if I never buy another book, the two free books and gifts are mine to keep forever.

154/354 HDN F4YN

Name _____ (PLEASE PRINT)

Address _____ Apt. #

City _____ State/Prov. _____ Zip/Postal Code

Signature (if under 18, a parent or guardian must sign)

Mail to the **Harlequin® Reader Service:**
IN U.S.A.: P.O. Box 1867, Buffalo, NY 14240-1867
IN CANADA: P.O. Box 609, Fort Erie, Ontario L2A 5X3

Want to try two free books from another line?
Call 1-800-873-8635 or visit www.ReaderService.com.

* Terms and prices subject to change without notice. Prices do not include applicable taxes. Sales tax applicable in N.Y. Canadian residents will be charged applicable taxes. Offer not valid in Quebec. This offer is limited to one order per household. Not valid for current subscribers to Harlequin American Romance books. All orders subject to credit approval. Credit or debit balances in a customer's account(s) may be offset by any other outstanding balance owed by or to the customer. Please allow 4 to 6 weeks for delivery. Offer available while quantities last.

Your Privacy—The Harlequin® Reader Service is committed to protecting your privacy. Our Privacy Policy is available online at www.ReaderService.com or upon request from the Harlequin Reader Service.

We make a portion of our mailing list available to reputable third parties that offer products we believe may interest you. If you prefer that we not exchange your name with third parties, or if you wish to clarify or modify your communication preferences, please visit us at www.ReaderService.com/consumerchoice or write to us at Harlequin Reader Service Preference Service, P.O. Box 9062, Buffalo, NY 14269. Include your complete name and address.

HAR13R

SPECIAL EXCERPT FROM

HARLEQUIN®

American Romance®

Read on for a sneak peek of
THE TEXAS CHRISTMAS GIFT
by Cathy Gillen Thacker

Eve Laughlin is completely unsentimental about
Christmas…until she meets the very attractive
Derek McCabe

This was what Eve wanted, too. Even if she would have preferred not to admit it. Before she could stop herself, before she could think of all the reasons why not, she let Derek pull her closer still. His head dipped. Her breath caught, and her eyes closed. And then all was lost in the first luscious feeling of his lips lightly pressed against hers.

It was a cautious kiss. A gentle kiss that didn't stay gallant for long. At her first quiver of sensation, he flattened his hands over her spine and deepened the kiss, seducing her with the heat of his mouth and the sheer masculinity of his tall, strong body. Yearning swept through her in great enervating waves. Unable to help herself, Eve went up on tiptoe, leaning into his embrace. Throwing caution to the wind, she wreathed her arms about his neck and kissed him back. Not tentatively, not sweetly, but with all the hunger and need she felt. And to her wonder and delight, he kissed her back in kind, again and again and again.

Derek had only meant to show Eve they had chemistry. Amazing chemistry that would convince her to go out with him, at least once. He hadn't expected to feel tenderness well inside him, even as his body went hard with desire. He hadn't expected to want to make love to her here and now, in this empty house. But sensing that total surrender would be a mistake, he tamped down his own desire and let the kiss come to a slow, gradual end.

Eve stepped backward, too, a mixture of surprise and pleasure on her face. Her breasts were rising and falling quickly, and her lips were moist. Amazement at the potency of their attraction, and something else a lot more cautious, appeared in her eyes. Eve drew a breath, and then anger flashed. "That was a mistake."

Derek understood her need to play down what had just happened, even as he saw no reason to pretend they hadn't enjoyed themselves immensely. "Not in my book," he murmured, still feeling a little off balance himself. In fact, he was ready for a whole lot more.

Can Derek convince Eve to take a chance
on him this Christmas?

Find out in
THE TEXAS CHRISTMAS GIFT
by Cathy Gillen Thacker
Available December 3, only from
Harlequin® American Romance®.

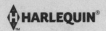

American Romance®

Since the first grade, Holly Johnson has known that
Ramon Rodriguez is the only man for her. But the carefree,
determinedly single Texas cowboy with the killer smile
doesn't have a clue. Until they share a dance and a kiss…
and Ray finally sees his best friend for the woman in love
she is. Now that he realizes what he's been missing,
Ray plans to make up for lost time…starting with the
three little words Holly's waited thirteen years to hear.

The Cowboy's Christmas Surprise
by *USA TODAY* bestselling author
MARIE FERRARELLA

Available November 5,
from Harlequin® American Romance®.

HAR75482